Stories and Lies

ALSO BY VERONICA ROSS

Hannah B.

Order in the Universe

Homecoming

Goodbye Summer

Dark Secrets

Fisherwoman

In the Carolyn Archer Mystery Series:

Millicent

The Anastasia Connection

The Burden of Grace

Stories and Lies

A CAROLYN ARCHER MURDER MYSTERY

VERONICA ROSS

THE MERCURY PRESS

The publisher gratefully acknowledges the financial assistance of the Canada Council for the Arts and the Ontario Arts Council, and further acknowledges the financial support of the Government of Canada through the Book Publishing Industry Development Program (BPIDP) for our publishing activities.

Canadä

Cover design by Gordon Robertson
Edited by Beverley Daurio
Composition and page design TASK

Printed and bound in Canada by Metropole Litho
Printed on acid-free paper
1 2 3 4 5   03 02 01 00 99

Canadian Cataloguing in Publication Data

Ross, Veronica
Stories and lies
"A Midnight Original murder mystery".
ISBN 1-55128-075-2
I. Title.
PS8585.O842S76 1999   C813'.54   C99-932061-0
PR9199.3.R67S76 1999

Represented in Canada by the Literary Press Group
Distributed in Canada by General Distribution Services

The Mercury Press
22 Prince Rupert Ave.
Toronto, Ontario
Canada   M6P 2A7

for Melissa

Chapter One

Roberta Kempton hadn't completed her assignment for Creative Writing 101.

"I'll just sit and listen." She was thin, fifty-something, with dyed blonde hair piled into an old-fashioned beehive. In three weeks of the ten week course, she had completed one assignment, a story about a dog. (*Write about a happy childhood memory,* I said. *Take it all in.*) I liked her story, which was funny and droll, but she was shy. Like the other students in the course, she wouldn't receive a credit. Courses offered by the Berlin Night School of the Arts were only for "life enrichment," as the brochure said.

I was teaching creative writing as a favour because the scheduled instructor, the poet Agnes Daumier, had broken her leg. I had the feeling that hiring Carolyn Archer, writer of popular mysteries and author of cookbooks, was considered a poor substitute for Agnes. But I was between books, and hey, why not teach? Maybe all that creativity generated by the philosophy of "art for everyone" would stimulate my own writing.

And, surprise, surprise, I enjoyed the class, enjoyed being "The Author"— the published writer, the magic genie who knew all the answers. I was having trouble starting a new novel and at times in the past year I'd wondered if the Muse had deserted me. So... the Carolyn Archer Admiration Society was a boost.

I loved the building, too— the old Berlin Academy where children had learned their ABCs for years, even way back before World War I when Kitchener was called Berlin and German was spoken on the streets. Gables, cupolas, broad staircases and tall windows made for an old world feel. It was fall and that early school earnestness of young scholars diligently listening to their teacher seemed present in my ten prospective writers, from nineteen-year-old Greg Theriault, who liked Sci Fi, to "seventy-plus and growing" Frederick Banners, a retired minister who was working on historical fiction. In between were Martha, Betsy, Roberta, Brad, Bron, Bella, Amanda, and Frances— storytellers, poets, family historians.

Already there was a feeling of closeness among them, of secrets and intimacies shared. I'd seen this before in other writing classes, but as I nodded at Roberta, I thought of the writing retreat up north that was part of the course. There was the lake beside the woods and... I must have frowned, because Roberta blushed and apologized for not doing her "homework."

"Better watch it or Teach'll give you a detention." Bella Pont was the class comedian and a writer of pungent stories about her misadventures with men. She was older than the other women, but that didn't deter her from looking like a vamp. Wild, red, frizzy hair framed round, cheerful cheeks. Green eye shadow and false eyelashes completed the picture.

"I'm only here for the enjoyment," Roberta said.

"That's why we're all here," I said easily. "You'll write when you can. Now, who's going to be the first to read?"

The assignment had been to write about a famous person, literary or otherwise, in a familiar setting. The week before I had read them a section from Timothy Findley's book about Joseph Conrad's Kurtz in Toronto. Several people had the paperback with them. Frances Harley, our critic, had post-it notes sticking from her copy, likely marking passages she disagreed with. Her lips were set in her thin face.

"I'll start." Brad Malkin cleared his throat and smiled. He was an executive at a computer firm, and writing a bestseller. "I made copies for everyone," he said, passing a stack of neatly stapled pages to his left before beginning his story about Marilyn Monroe visiting his condo while his wife attended her aerobics class. He cleared his throat and brushed back his layered hair. Handsome boy: with his carefully casual blue linen shirt he could have posed for BMW ads.

"My hands trembled as I passed her a cocktail. Marilyn was a vision to behold, the most gorgeous woman I had ever seen, a phantom in white. After giving her the cocktail, I could see her breasts heaving through the thin fabric of her halter top. As she lifted her glass, I felt the beginning of erotic bliss..."

The classroom door opened and Amanda Gray tiptoed in. "Sorry," she mouthed, as she slid into a chair and tossed her grey-blonde hair back.

She unbuttoned her handwoven jacket. She was theriter here and I loved her stories about her mentally ill mother.

"...her hand fell on my thigh. She paused befog, 'You work out. I'd love to see you in a bathing suit.' After drinkply of the red liquid in her glass, she asked provocatively, 'Why ou show me your bedroom?'"

"Hope you tidied up!" Bella laughed.

"We tiptoed up the stairs together and turned rigthe bedroom. Stretching out on the pink coverlet, Marilyn began uing my white shirt. Suddenly, I heard my wife's car entering the g

Wife rushes in and socks Marilyn on the nose. n pulls wife's hair. Wife is stronger and wrestles Marilyn to the flod is just going to throw cold water on the women when Marilyn'sl spills on the white rug and the wife runs for the rug shampooeryn disappears into the night and Brad's wife makes him clean the

Silence.

"Thanks, Brad. I really liked the humour at th I said. "The rather frantic energy worked well." The story was prle and I could see cuts in the transitions, but I always began with somencouraging. Later, I'd do editing on my copy of his story. "You amost start the story at the end, work back from there."

"Start at the climax!" Bella said.

Frederick's eyes twinkled. He resembled Gregck. "On page three... right at the top... I'd suggest taking out the vreathlessly.'"

"What kind of cocktail was it?" Martha Caplaed to know. "Because some stains never come out." She was ant, motherly woman who attended with her best friend, Betsy (rs. Betsy and Martha had been writing stories together for years. even looked alike, pleasant women with neat brown hairdos.

Bella said to send it to *Playboy*.

Greg grinned.

"I just loved the story!"

"It depends on the kind of shampoo you use."

"Not if the rug is synthetic."

"Is Brg to follow Marilyn to Hollywood?"

"Mariuld be old by now. Seventy or something. You could have her to a crone like in— what's that story where the young girl turns iold hag when they get to Tibet?"

"Did ife read the story?"

Francey said she was tired of stories about adultery.

This o on forever. "Let's move to the next story," I said, and nodded at la, who didn't have enough copies for everyone. I had a hunch hey was tight. She'd had a buy-out from the bank where she'd work long time the year before and that money was probably dwindling

"I'm sout the copies," she said, and began. She was shy at first and her vavered, but soon she was lost in the story.

"My was mad that Wednesday. She had set the table with Grandmotory linen, the sterling cutlery and gold dishes. Candles, candy disrared pink and green almonds, the white teapot. Snow outside. Ine paced to the tick-tock, tick-tock of the grandfather clock. Gahe air, the good smell of lamb and rosemary. 'Ronald Reagan's for dinner!' she told me as I removed my boots. It had been on th news, she said, that Ronald Reagan was visiting her for dinnerCBC news truck had driven by twice. Soon the world would kntruth!

"My brown leather lace-ups. I had been foolish to buy them and the lack under my cold fingers in that air of garlic and madness while Man Helen looked over my shoulder for the white stretch limo that deliver her love, her true husband, through the snow. The city seike Pompeii: the snow would bury us. And the smashed porcelain and the rosemary gravy on the floor. Tears and sobs while ruin fell, stlike the snow..."

Bella even have a wisecrack.

The class Thursday nights and some students went to the Walper Hotel aftelass, for beer and talk at the Berlin Circle, an arts and letters club, but I had an early morning television interview in Kitchener and I had to drive Bronwen home to the other end of Guelph.

Bron had once been married to my friend, Neil Andersen. Neil and I had been— almost— more than friends. After being happily married to Peter Hall for more than ten years, I had suddenly, unexpectedly, found myself attracted to Neil. But the issue became a non-issue when Bron moved in again with Neil.

They had been divorced for years and their daughter was grown. Neil had had a live-in girlfriend for a while, but when I met him he was living by himself. He never talked much about his marriage until Bron reappeared in his life.

"As they used to say, we had to marry," Neil explained. "For years Bron claimed I'd only married her because I had to. It sounds so stupid today."

Bron started drinking as she and Neil moved from small town to small town because of Neil's work with the Ontario Provincial Police. It was a long, sad story of fights and reconciliations, and finally they divorced. Neil got custody of their daughter, Maureen.

But after their separation, Bron attended AA, regained custody of Maureen, enrolled in a nursing assistant course and graduated with honours. Things might have been fine if her boyfriend hadn't died of a massive coronary. Bron started drinking again, smashed her car up, and lost her job. When Neil learned she was living in a room in Toronto, he offered to let her live in his house until she got on her feet.

Bron jumped at the chance to take my course. She was heavy-set and plain in a countrywoman sort of way, and read big historical romances and true stories about women who conquered difficulties. Her face was puffy, and her beige hair was lopped off, but it was easy to see the snub-nosed blonde she had once been.

She planned to write about her drinking problem, but the assignments led to quirky stories about Graingerville, where she lived when she met Neil.

She could only attend my class if I drove her. She had lost her license.

"I really liked your story about the McMullin sisters," I told her on the way back to Guelph. "I loved the way you left that bit of mystery."

"Well, no one really knew much about them. They moved to town when they retired— and no one moved to Graingerville. Why were they there? That's what everyone wanted to find out. It was terrible, setting their fence on fire on Hallowe'en. Then someone poisoned their dog. And the younger one was accused of shoplifting, but she had a receipt from another store in her purse."

"The tone reminded me of a Shirley Jackson story," I said. "'The Lottery.' But in that story there's not really a reason for what happens."

"I'll have to look the story up in the library. So much to read," Bron sighed. "I'm still on Timothy Findley."

"You should try Robertson Davies for small town gothic."

I started to relate the story of *Fifth Business*— how boys threw a snowball and knocked down a pregnant woman, which changed everyone's life, but... what had happened in the book? It was years since I'd read it and... I tried to remember as I focused on the dark road. Kitchener was only a good half-hour from Guelph, but the highway was dark. Bron was talking about the story she planned to work on, something about a neighbour whose husband locked her out, but her voice sounded distant. "A snowfall that night"... "no boots"... "threatened to sue if anyone took her in." Her handbag, placed squarely on her ample lap, looked enormous, and lights of the strip malls as we neared Guelph seemed far away. Suddenly I was thinking of Maine, where I had grown up, of foggy nights and the mournful wail of the buoys... Matthew Arnold's "Dover Beach"... "the turbid ebb and flow/of human misery."

"Well, I've missed our coffee," Bron said as I turned the corner to Neil's place. "Sure you can't come in for a tea or something? Neil will still be at that stag."

"I wish I could, but I'll be up at the crack of dawn to make myself gorgeous for the camera," I said, although what I really wanted was to be at home with Peter and our Labrador retriever, Conrad.

"Too bad you have to turn around and go back to Kitchener in the morning. If it wasn't for me, you could have stayed over and..."

She didn't continue. Flashing lights from police cars filled the autumn night air and a body was being removed from the house next to Neil's. Yellow police ribbons had been set up. Neighbours, all in a huddle, stood watch across Neil's ordinary suburban street, Bricker Crescent, with its lawns and back-splits illuminated by red arcs of light. As the medics loaded the covered still form into the ambulance, a streak of light caught the faces on the sidewalk: white and hushed and still. A woman dabbed at her eyes.

The ambulance shrieked as it tore away.

Chapter Two

The dead person was Maria Maloff, aged 81. Immigrant, hoer of cabbages and pruner of roses, lonely widow, and doting grandmother of Burton— Burton the biker— who harassed and begged and pleaded for hand-outs and who, the week before, had been hauled away by the police from Grandma's house, where he had raised holy hell. Burton, son of Suzanne, hooker and stripper, widow of Maria's son, John, a long-distance hauler who had met his end on a wet road in Illinois.

Maria: a little woman who waved to me from her vegetable patch. Neil shovelled her walk in the winter and drove her to the doctor.

The police told Neil, officer to officer, that Maria had been shot through the head.

"Some people have more suffering than they deserve," Neil said in his kitchen. "Poor old Maria. If only she'd pressed charges against her grandson. The punk would have been behind bars. Any tea left?" he asked Bron, but poured himself a cup before she could get up to check. "Poor old woman. He wanted money from her last week and when she said no, he threatened to burn her house down. Doper. You know the saying about selling your own grandmother. That's Burton."

He looked tired. His eyes didn't crinkle, and his skin was white under the kitchen light.

Bron lit a smoke.

"Maybe he didn't do it," I said.

"Oh, he did it all right. They'll get him."

"Spoken like a true cop," I said. "What about innocent until proven guilty?"

"I've known too many dopers in my time. Nah. I've known Burton for years. He lived there for a year when the authorities took him from his mother. His grandfather kept him in line, though. The old man would be inside yelling and poor Maria would be weeding her cabbages and crying. The only grandchild. The son dead."

"Why did they remove Burton from his mother?"

"She was hooking, bootlegging, you name it. Burton was ten or eleven. Stealing bicycles. He stole my lawnmower, come to think of it, but his grandfather made him return it. Stole money out of Maria's purse to buy cigarettes. Maria was a pushover. After the old man died, the only time Burton came by to visit was when he wanted money from her."

"So he went back to his mother," I said.

"The old folks tried to fight it, but there was nothing they could do. I always liked Maria. She reminded me of Ukrainian women out west. She kept to herself, but we became friends after her husband died. All she ever wanted was her home and family, and family did her in at the end. It's a sad story."

"It looks to me as if Burton never had a chance," I said, and glanced at my watch. "I should go. I have that television interview in Kitchener at nine tomorrow morning. I'll have to be up at six and I know I won't be able to get to sleep."

"Too much tea and murder," Neil said. "That'll do it."

Neil walked me to my car while Bron put the mugs into the dishwasher.

"I'm going to go home and have a drink," I told him. He nodded to the two officers in the cruiser. A van marked "Identification" was in the driveway.

"Sorry I couldn't oblige, but with Bron on the wagon... you know how it is. How's she doing in your class?"

"Great. She seems to be enjoying it."

"Thanks for driving her. I know it's an inconvenience." He pointed at the wrapped shrubs on Maria's lawn. "I wonder who'll be unwrapping them in the spring?"

I encountered Conrad and Peter as I turned onto Lancaster Street in downtown Guelph. As usual, Conrad was taking Peter for a walk. Peter lurched behind, his hair all over the place and his glasses sliding down his nose as he tried to control Conrad, who was foraging for something edible in the grass. I shouldn't have tooted the horn. With a heave, Conrad jerked the leash out of Peter's grip.

"Conrad, you asshole," Peter said as Conrad scrambled into the back of the Volvo and stepped on my briefcase. "What a dog! You're late, aren't you? Allison called. We're getting the kids this weekend. She's off to Kingston to visit Steven."

Allison's fiancé, Steven MacLeod, was serving four years for impersonating a doctor. Steven was a male nurse from Scotland. Allison had met him when he was the "doctor" in her home town, Meredith, in northern Ontario. Now Allison was going to be the doctor.

"So I said, sure, the kids are welcome. We don't have anything planned for this weekend. Did you?" Peter asked as I pulled in front of our old stone house on Lancaster. Two years before a meddling friend had told him lies about me and Neil, but now that Bron was back with Neil, Peter had dismissed that concern.

"Pour me a glass of vino," I called, settling on the couch while Peter gave Conrad his nightly dog cookie in the kitchen, "and I'll tell you why I'm late."

It was a quarter to eight when I awoke the next morning. There was time only to wash with cold water and put on a bit of make-up. My hair looked lacklustre, not frizzy and fluffy, but at least my purple, artsy dress was all right. By ten after eight I was on the road to Kitchener.

Highway 7 was busy with people heading to work, and it was ten to nine when I pulled into the parking lot of CKPQ. The make-up person gave me a quick brush with powder before Lindsey Newman, looking like a take-charge businesswoman in her fawn suit, hustled me into the studio.

"Late night, was it?" Her eyes glinted beneath her helmet of auburn hair.

I'd been interviewed on television many times and I was usually not nervous, but Lindsey made me feel like a snivelling schoolgirl.

"Don't be jittery, now. The program's live, but you can always kill yourself if it turns out badly. What have you done to your hair? It was fuller before."

There was no time to answer. Lindsey settled herself comfortably in her green armchair and we were on the air.

"Good morning, good morning! I have with me this beautiful fall day Carolyn Archer, Guelph's answer to Agatha Christie, who literally just flew into the studio minutes before air time! I am so relieved to have you here, Carolyn. Tell us why you were late!"

"Traffic was slow," I mumbled at Lindsey's glittering smile.

"Next time we'll send a limo, as I'm sure they do in New York. Because, ladies and gentlemen, Carolyn Archer has been on the major television networks! She is the creme de la creme of mystery writers, and a writer who apparently does not believe in the old saying that those who can, do, and those who can't, teach."

It got worse. I mumbled and fidgeted and at one point found myself running my fingers through my not-great hair. Didn't I consider it a comedown to be teaching at night school? Did I think I would discover a Hemingway, a Joyce Carol Oates? Had I sold out, writing mysteries? Where did I get ideas for all those gruesome stories?

"I read things, the newspapers, like, you know," I stumbled. Suddenly I felt a big yawn coming. I was going to yawn; nothing would stop it.

But instead of yawning, I was telling Lindsey about "a grandmother murdered by her grandson."

What? What?

"I believe there was a story about that very thing on the news this morning!" Lindsey opened her eyes wide. "They arrested a suspect."

"I'm afraid I didn't catch the news this morning..."

At last we were off the air. As I removed the mike from the collar of my dress, Lindsey asked if I'd ever thought of taking valium before "a performance."

Amanda Gray in her famous jacket was waiting for me in the lobby. She looked— writerly. That was the word to describe her. An intelligent, angular face framed by well-cut dark blonde hair with hints of premature grey. No make-up. Her greenish eyes were alert and bright, rueful when she saw my expression.

"I have just had the most ghastly experience of my life," I told her, as if I'd known her forever. "That Lindsey is a certified bitch."

"That bad? I was on television once— a street interview— and I looked like a washerwoman. Want a coffee?"

"I'd love a coffee. Breakfast, too."

"How did you know I was going to invite you for breakfast? Come on, we'll go in my car. I have this little hole in the wall where I go to write sometimes. You can pick up your car later. You look frazzled."

After the poisonous Lindsey, it felt wonderful to be with Amanda in a tiny lunchroom in Kitchener's downtown. Red arborite tables, a chalkboard offering hot turkey sandwiches, and a gossipy waitress who knew Amanda and immediately brought the coffee pot soon put me at ease.

"I love this place," Amanda said. "There are all the trendy cafés up the street, but I can sit here all day and be inspired. Feel part of life. Family people as well as the weirdos the city fathers are trying to get off the street. But they're all people with stories. See that guy there?" She indicated a thin man leaning against a wall across the street. "That's Johnny. In the summer he works on the Mennonite farms, but come fall he settles into his room and hangs around. When his welfare cheque comes he goes on his monthly drunk and sometimes the cops pick him up, but he's harmless. I'd like to do a series of stories about the downtown people if I ever finish that thing about my mother."

"You're full of ideas," I said, slicing a thick rasher of crisp bacon.

"You'll sell what you're writing now. I'm sure of it. Perhaps not for much money at first, but you can collect the stories and have a book published. I think your writing is wonderful."

"You don't know what it means to me when you say that. I should have done what I had to do long ago."

"It must have been difficult, with your mother."

"It was after Dad died. The only alternative was to put her into an institution. My father was great. I don't know how he coped, but I had a more-or-less normal childhood. When Mom had her spells he'd find something special to do— maybe walking in the park or making a doll house out of a cardboard box with me. Even when I became a teenager, he was the one who coped with her. But all that changed when he died of a heart attack. I had just turned eighteen. I was supposed to go to university that fall."

"You didn't go?"

"I took courses here and there, but it all became too much. Mom would decide to run away or lock herself in the bathroom on the day of exams and I'd get an F. It was all I could do to cope with my job, clean and cook at home. And later there were bank courses. Deadly dull stuff, but they helped me get ahead."

"And then you lost your job."

"That was a blessing in disguise. The separation package was pretty decent and I sold the house in Scarborough and moved here. I can live for years on my savings."

"Somehow I thought you were from Kitchener."

"Dad's family was from here. I spent a few summers here as a kid. The old aunts are gone, but I have a couple of cousins I see at funerals and weddings."

"Too bad your father didn't move back."

"Not a good idea. Mom stabbed Beulah, his eldest sister, with Beulah's sewing scissors. It's one of my earliest memories. I was four or five. We were here for another aunt's birthday and the kids were playing in the back yard. Beulah asked me if I wanted a sun hat— the sun was beating down— and Mom interpreted that as criticism and interference.

Beulah kept the scissors in her mother's old Singer treadle machine at the top of the stairs."

I dipped the last of my toast into the runny egg. More coffee appeared. "I needed this," I said.

"If you ever want a place to write, come here."

"I haven't written in restaurants for years. I used to do that in Guelph to get away from my ex."

I told her about Charlie, who was abusive and awful. He disappeared years before, when I was involved with the story of my friend, Millicent Mulvey, who claimed to have been married to the Duke of Windsor before the famous Wallis Simpson snagged him.

Amanda said she'd been engaged once, but the man couldn't cope with her mother.

"Well, now you're free," I said. "You can do anything you want to do."

"I think it's *have to do*," Amanda said. "There are things I have to do. Writing."

We sat over our coffee and watched the street. A blonde woman in skin-tight jeans lolled on the corner. A cigarette dangled from her bright lips. She wasn't too young.

"A hooker," Amanda said. "She doesn't have a purse. They never carry purses. I don't know who she is, though."

"The guy I told you about, Burton, whom I stupidly mentioned on the show, although, thank goodness I didn't use his name— I wasn't quite that rattled— his mother's a hooker. Or was."

"Some of them are just kids," Amanda said. "Troubled young girls on crack. Anyway, anyway... I can hardly wait to go on that retreat up north. I've never been on one. It sounds so... poetic."

"You'll love the lodge. It's owned by friends of my in-laws and it's a really neat place, right on the lake. Wonderful decor, paintings and quilts. We usually go there for New Year's Eve. It's one of the most peaceful places in the universe. And the food is superb."

"The price is right, too. A three-day vacation for two hundred dollars. I can hardly wait."

"Same here," I said.

There were five messages on the machine when I got back to Guelph, four from students who had watched *Breakfast with Lindsey*. Roberta congratulated me; Frederick remarked that Lindsey would have been burned at the stake not too long ago; Betsy said shyly, "I just wanted you to know that I watched your program"; and Bella drawled, "It sure wasn't NBC." My friend, Emma, suggested we get together soon.

The phone rang while I was listening to messages.

A husky female voice said, "You think you're smart, don't you?"

Chapter Three

I was flabbergasted when Peter's sister, Allison, announced that she had been accepted into the medical program at Chedoke-McMaster Hospital in Hamilton. From housewife to medical doctor was a long road. I hated the word "housewife," but how else to describe Allison who, for years, had been unhappily married to Joe in Meredith? Allison's life had been bound by Meredith's gossip and way of life. Joe was a huntin' and fishin' type of guy. Allison married him soon after high school, had three children in six years, and spent her days chain-smoking, picking up after Joe, yelling at the kids, and complaining.

Her and Peter's parents, Marion and Hugh Hall, were from England and had been in Meredith for over thirty years. They had wanted more for their kids. At least Peter had gone to university and eventually opened a bookstore in Guelph. After Hugh retired as Chief of Police, they started a bed and breakfast.

When Allison left Joe—a long drawn-out affair, including a stay with us in Guelph, she enrolled in a Registered Nursing course. And became engaged to her Scottish "doctor." After two years of nursing, she had been accepted into the medical program at McMaster.

Dr. Allison Hall?

"I certainly appreciate you taking the kids for the weekend," she said to me Friday evening. "It's going to be a busy month and if I don't get away now, who knows when I can get to Kingston to see Steven?"

"She might as well just dump us here," Matthew said. "So I can get to drive you crazy."

At almost fifteen, he was my favourite of Allison's boys. Timmy and Jody were great, but Matthew and I had a special bond. He had had his hair spiked, but the old grin was the same.

"Take over the computer," he added.

"I'll computer you," Allison said brusquely. The awful variations of make-up she'd tried in the past years were gone. Her hair was clipped, making her look adolescent and seriously grown-up at the same time. I could almost picture her in a white coat, with a stethoscope dangling around her neck. "Dr. Hall wanted in Emergency! Paging Dr. Hall!"

"You know Carolyn has to write," she told Matthew. Once, this thought would never have occurred to her.

"Didn't I hear something about writers' block?" Matthew asked.

"Go see what the little hellions are doing," Allison said.

"They're watching someone getting shot on TV."

"Go, go!"

"It's no trouble at all to keep the boys," I said after Matthew joined Timmy and Jody in the living room. "Any time at all."

"So I can visit my convict?" Allison frowned. "Mom and Dad say I should dump him. They think I was only attracted to him because he was the big doc. So now I'll be the big doc. I bet you thought I'd dump the guy, too."

She didn't wait for me to answer.

"It was Steven's idea I try at Mac. If it weren't for Steven I probably would have dropped out of nursing. He's still the same person."

"What about when he gets out?"

"In two years, three at the most. He should get early parole and by then I'll be getting to the end at Mac. He'll almost be through his university correspondence courses by then. In the meantime it's off for conjugal visits. To the trailer I go." She glanced at her watch. "I should get on the road. It'll be eleven before I get to Kingston."

"Say hello to Steven. I always liked him."

"Everyone did," Allison said. "We'll probably get married while he's still in prison."

Somehow, I doubted that.

Later, I took the boys to Pizza Hut. Peter was at his bookstore, The Bookworm, and I thought of dropping in, but Jody and Timmy clamoured for videos. We took Conrad for a run, and by the time Peter came home, the younger kids were watching a Benji movie and Matthew was surfing our new Internet.

Maybe Matthew was right; perhaps I really did have writers' block, I thought, as I started reading the students' handed-in assignments.

I did a lot of line-editing on Brad's story, re-read a juvenile story about Santa Claus, and turned, with some relief, to a story Amanda hadn't read in class. The limit was one story per student a week, but Amanda was writing more and more, and I tacitly accepted her extra work.

It was a wonderful story about Amanda trying to get away for a weekend. Her mother cut her hair off. Amanda kept packing. She put her coat by the door. Her mother disappeared.

It would have been a victim's story, but it was saved by fantasy. By the time she located her mother, Amanda was, in her head, on a journey to Europe. The imaginary journey was told in a realistic, journalistic way— couples talking in train stations, a whining child, a peasant woman carrying a large suitcase. Mini-stories in a larger story.

At the end, Amanda wove in her mother's journey. "Mrs. Gray settled herself on the bench. She was waiting for the train to Budapest..."

Teaching the course was worth it, just to be able to read Amanda's work.

In the morning, the weather was crisp and clear, an almost Indian summer day. It was a day to be outside, and I called my friend, Emma, who owned Conrad's sister, Kelly, to see if she wanted to visit our old friend, Scottie McGrath, and run the dogs. We were almost out of the door when Bron called. She was feeling rotten, old allergies acting up. She didn't know where Neil was. He was gone when she awoke.

I could hear her wheezing. Between gasps she told me she had no money on her for a taxi. She had to get to the hospital for oxygen.

"I'll be right there," I said.

I phoned Emma, who agreed to pick the kids and Conrad up. I'd meet her at Scottie's after I had taken Bron to the hospital. It was a hopeful plan. I couldn't just dump Bron off at Emergency and speed away.

But unkindly thoughts fled when I found Bron, gasping for air, sitting on her doorstep. Her face was flushed and her eyes were swollen. There was a button missing on her red jacket, which was too short for her grey sweatshirt.

"Maybe we should call an ambulance?"

"Just need... it's happened before..."

I held the car door open for her. She put her head back, and took long, deep breaths. I had read a story somewhere about a pioneer woman with pneumonia, who had hung to life by concentrating on each breath. In-out, in-out. Bron was like that as I raced her to the hospital.

Bron's breathing eased in the waiting room. By the time a doctor saw her ten minutes later, she was almost breathing normally. "It must be something in the house," she mumbled as she followed the nurse. "I swear there's a cat hidden in there."

I was reading about developing good sleep habits in a tattered *Reader's Digest*, when Bron, looking much better, emerged clutching a prescription.

"I have to get a puffer," she told me. "I'm supposed to go for allergy tests. And he said I should quit smoking.

"And right now I want a cigarette more than anything," she added as we walked out of the hospital.

Neil's car was in the driveway when we got back. He had gone to the airport to pick up Mrs. Maloff's sister, Mrs. Schultz, who was drinking tea in the kitchen. She had a broad, weathered face and wore a tight blue suit. Neil had invited her to stay with them until after Maria's funeral, which would be the following Monday.

She was also cradling an orange and white cat.

"Willy," Neil explained. "I guess Mrs. Maloff— your sister," he told Mrs. Schultz, "must have let the cat out and it sneaked inside here when no one answered his meows next door. Poor little fellow." He patted the cat's head. Willy hissed at him, jumped off Mrs. Schultz's lap, and darted down the basement stairs.

Mrs. Schultz took a white handkerchief out of her purse and dabbed her eyes. "He came right out when I arrived. He must have remembered me. Poor Willy," she sighed. She had only a very slight accent and seemed younger than the old woman I had seen working in the garden.

Neil shook his head. "Looks like we've got ourselves a cat. For now, anyway."

Obviously Neil had forgotten Bron's allergy. I spoke up and explained about Bron's trip to the hospital.

"But that is terrible!" Mrs. Schultz said. "I cannot take the cat. In my building it is not allowed."

"I'll take him," I said. "Until we figure something out."

But first we had to catch him. Neil found him, finally, behind the dryer. Willy darted away and hid under an old couch. Finally, Mrs. Schultz managed to coax him out, and Neil fetched a cardboard box.

"What's Conrad going to say?" he asked. "Poor cat'll be his dinner, probably."

I had a sudden inspiration. I would take Willy to The Bookworm!

Peter was not amused.

"Why on earth would anyone have a cat? You know how Conrad loves chasing cats."

Peter reached a tentative hand to the cat, who hissed and slashed the air with his claws before disappearing behind cartons of unpacked books.

"He'll go right for Conrad's eyes, and then what?"

"It's only for a while. He can hide out in the back of the store. There should be some milk in the fridge."

Neil had gone over to Mrs. Maloff's for cat food and the litter box, which now sat by Peter's desk.

"I have never liked cats," Peter said. "It acts like it has rabies, too."

"Don't fuss so much. It won't be for long. We'll find him a home, put an ad in the paper."

"There is no way Conrad will put up with a cat. Never, never."

"Conrad will never meet Mr. Willy. Just keep the office door shut or he'll dart out."

Conrad knew immediately that a cat had been in the car. The dogs were still racing around with the kids when I got to Scottie's place, but Conrad dashed right to our car and jumped into the front seat, where the cardboard box containing the cat had been. Labradors are super sniffers in the dog world and if Conrad was an expert at finding discarded apples and bones, he was a pro at tracing the feline scent. Sniff, sniff, pant, pant. He circled and snuffled and gave me an incredulous look. A cat, in his car? What was I doing with a cat? He barked sharply at me and pawed at the seat covers as if he might find a tiger inside.

Maybe Emma would take Willy? She and Mark already had one cat, Pumpkin, and they lived in the country. But Kelly only tolerated poor Pumpkin...

"If you are really, absolutely stuck," she said uncertainly in Scottie's kitchen, "I guess we can put him up for a while. He can stay in the studio."

Emma was a quilt-maker and she'd recently renovated the old barn and turned it into a studio. Her photo had been on the cover of *Guelph Monthly* recently: an artist with a blonde Dutch bob against a backdrop of a picture quilt of a woman sewing.

To my surprise, Scottie wasn't too keen on taking in a cat. He was going to Scotland for Christmas, he said, and Johnny from down the road was already looking after Lady...

(Excuses, excuses...)

...and he was off weekends to visit Mother... (his mother, Mabel, had been in prison, but was now in a psychiatric hospital) and with his work... and he'd never really "been a one for cats."

No one was interested in an orphaned cat!

Even a cat orphaned by the murder of his mistress. There was some tut-tutting. Scottie and Emma had heard about Burton's arrest on the evening news, but neither had known Maria.

Or did mention of any murder remind Scottie of what had happened to his mother?

Was that why he wouldn't take the cat?

"You are going, then? It's decided? You've definitely made up your mind?" Emma asked Scottie.

"Yes, indeed I have. I'll have an early Christmas visit with Mother and then it's over the briny sea I go!" He reached for a cookie, or biscuit as he called it. Mabel would have served homemade scones. The kitchen was the same, with its old arborite table and white curtains, but I always expected Mabel to step into the kitchen and briskly remove her apron. Poor Mabel. She had not been able to accept her son's homosexuality and this had led to the murder of a neighbour.

"All the arrangements are made," Scottie added and grinned. He was small, but wiry. His old-fashioned, short haircut made him look boyish. He wore a garish turquoise sweater— Mabel wouldn't have allowed that. "I will be staying with Mother's cousin."

"And we are going to Holland for Christmas," Emma told me.

"Everyone's travelling. What a surprise!" I said and looked at Emma, who seemed so happy these days. Her face glowed beneath her blonde hair. She was one of my oldest friends in the Guelph area. I had met her when I was still married to Charlie and she was living in the country at Mark's commune. Mark and Emma had gone their separate ways, met again when Emma returned with her son, Thomas, from Holland, and then married quickly.

She and Mark had gone through a bad spell. There were problems with Mark accepting Thomas, but after they went for counselling, everything worked out. Her growing fame as a quilt designer helped. The summer before, Emma had spent a month at an art workshop in Arizona. Mark had really missed her.

"Did you say the cat's name was Willy?" Emma asked suddenly. "I had a cat called Willy when I was a kid. My parents never had him fixed. He was always tomming around. One day he left and never came back."

"And a cat that's not fixed will be tomming around, all right. And spraying and scratching the furniture and what have you!" Scottie said.

"I want to see the cat!" Jody demanded. "Can we go see the cat, Carolyn?"

"Conrad'll eat him up!" Timmy chortled.

The boys had had a cat when Allison and Joe were still together, but it had been run over by a car.

Would Allison take the cat? I wondered.

But the cat was nowhere to be seen in The Bookworm, where we stopped after buying milk and bread. Willy seemed to have disappeared. He wasn't behind the packing cases and he wasn't hiding in the store. The boys couldn't find him in the dark basement where Peter kept cartons of secondhand books that hadn't been priced yet. The water and dry cat food hadn't been touched and the litter box was clean.

"Are you sure the cat didn't sneak out?" I asked Peter. "You kept the office door shut?"

Peter swore the door had remained closed.

"I bet Peter sort of forgot to shut the door," Jody mused on the way home. "He hates cats."

The cat was still missing by the time of Mrs. Maloff's funeral on Monday.

"I have a favour to ask," Bron said. "Neil invited everyone back here after the funeral. And I was wondering if you could come over and sort of set up the teacups and things. He's got platters of deli ordered and cakes and stuff. I'd stay here myself but Juliana wants me to go to the funeral. I don't see how I can get out of going."

Juliana Schultz and her sister, Maria Maloff, Bron explained on the phone, had been ethnic Germans in Russia who escaped to Germany, where they met their husbands at refugee camps before coming to Canada.

"Juliana was her only family," Bron said. "Juliana didn't have any kids and both the husbands are dead. There's only Burton, but naturally he won't be there. It's so sad. They had a big farm in Russia before the revolution, but they still had the house when they fled. They had to leave everything behind. Juliana has some cousins in Russia she hasn't seen for over fifty years. She's been sending them parcels and money."

Sad, sad, I agreed, and said of course I'd come over to the house and set things up.

"Frankly, I'll be glad when Juliana's gone. It turns out she's executrix of her sister's will, but I'm hoping she'll move next door after the funeral. I spent yesterday going through her sister's house with her. All those ornaments and dishes. Juliana gets keepsakes and the dining-room set, but the proceeds of the sale of the rest were going to go to Burton. I guess if he's guilty of killing his grandmother, Juliana gets everything."

"You sound tired, Bron."

"I've been listening to stories for two days now. It's not so bad, she has to talk, and it's interesting. But she wants to sit up all night. She really hates Burton and his mother. She had his mother barred from the funeral. I hope there won't be a scene. She's afraid Burton will get off and then his mother will 'steal everything,' as she says. Juliana's convinced that the mother— Suzanne— will turn up at the funeral. Neil says the TV people will be there. Maria didn't have a lot of friends, but people will be curious. Juliana wants Suzanne arrested if she turns up."

"It sounds as if you have your hands full."

"My ears full is more like it. Neil asked me if I minded about having the reception here, but it's strictly his show. He would have called you himself but he and Juliana are at the funeral home right now. She soaks her feet every night and can't use salt on her food, but she eats piles of salami and liver sausage!"

"Sounds like fun."

"She's afraid Suzanne will break into her sister's house during the funeral, but I think the police are sending a cruiser to guard the place. She wants to write a book about Russia and the war, by the way. Neil made the mistake of telling her about you and the class. I hope she won't want to join the course if she stays on for a bit."

"Tell her registration's over."

"She's a very determined woman," Bron said.

Grief seemed to have fled as Juliana, dressed in funereal navy and stout shoes and matching heavy leather bag, warned me about the "terrible Suzanne" as soon as I arrived. A woman without morals, education and background had inveigled her sister's only son, John, into marriage. Suzanne had forbidden John to visit his parents; she had insulted his mother, and kept the grandparents from their only grandson. Poor John had no choice but to obey his wife and Juliana was certain his home life was the cause of the accident that killed him.

"She will cause trouble, you will see," Juliana said, as she pulled on leather gloves. "I know it. Anything not nailed down she will steal and sell for money for drugs."

"The police will watch the house," Neil assured her. He looked handsome in his dark suit. Bron wore her usual polyester pants, but she'd added a red blazer and white blouse. And high heels, clump clump. She tottered on them. The air smelled of cigarette smoke. "We should get going," Neil said, glancing at his watch.

"She will be arrested if she turns up at the funeral," Juliana told me. "That woman belongs in jail along with her son!"

There was not much to do. Platters of cold cuts, bread and cheese, covered with plastic wrap, sat on the kitchen table and Bron had already unpacked the rented cups and saucers. The coffee-maker was ready to be plugged in and I only had to make tea. There were also plates of cookies and brownies.

A large, unopened bottle of Seagram's V.O. stood on the counter. Was this one of the reasons Bron had wanted me to stay here? I wondered as I rinsed glasses, uncovered the platters, set out the cups and looked for paper napkins, which I was unable to find. There were four red cloth napkins in the linen closet but those wouldn't go far. I folded paper towels into squares and discovered a new box of tissues in the bathroom vanity. Within ten minutes, I had everything ready except the tea.

Before Bron's arrival, I had only been in Neil's place a few times. Once, I had dropped Conrad off for Neil to babysit when Peter and I went to Ottawa for the weekend. I had come by one Saturday morning to return the jacket Neil forgot at our place and we sat in the kitchen and drank instant coffee and Conrad was sick on the living-room rug.

It was not an interesting place. His girlfriend must have removed any decorative touches when she left, I thought. The living room was dominated by a television set, stereo components in make-your-own shelving and Neil's big chair. A framed Robert Bateman picture hung over the gold sofa. A striped blue loveseat sat in what was supposed to be the dining area. A spindly philodendron trailed over a macramé plant holder.

Downstairs, in the never-used rec room, Juliana's green suitcase sat beside the pull-out couch. There was another television, a vinyl bar, and an empty fireplace.

Washer, dryer, pantyhose and Bron's red sweatshirt drying on a rack, piles of newspapers bundled for recycling and winter boots. A shower stall.

People in stories always open medicine cabinets, I thought as I combed my hair in the upstairs bathroom. Down the hall were the three bedrooms. The doors were closed. The nearest was Neil's. I inched the door open. There was a bookcase stuffed with paperbacks, a green plaid shirt lying on the bed. I shut the door and returned to the kitchen, where I plugged in the kettle.

The cruiser was still on the street, and Willy the cat was on Mrs. Maloff's doorstep, staring balefully at the front door.

I was dialling The Bookworm when the funeral cars returned. There were only a dozen people: two men and their wives, dressed in sombre black, who had worked with Joseph, Maria's late husband; the practical nurse, a very fat woman in a brown pantsuit, who had come to cut Mrs. Maloff's toenails; three neighbours, and, of course, Bron, Neil and Juliana. Why on earth had Neil bothered with rented cups?

"Thank goodness the press didn't come," Neil said, pouring himself an inch of whiskey while Bron and Juliana passed food around in the living room. "A lot of curious people, though."

"How was the funeral? The infamous Suzanne didn't appear?"

"Nope." He swallowed his drink and closed his eyes. "I think Juliana was disappointed. The funeral was sad. The priest didn't know Maria. He couldn't even say she was a proud grandmother. He talked about her hard time in the war, her coming to Canada. Her devotion! I spoke about having her as a neighbour, her love of her home and her garden."

"You gave the eulogy? I didn't know you were going to do that."

"Who else? She was a nice woman. She didn't deserve to die the way she did. She never asked for much out of life. God, I hate these stinking family tragedies. And little jerks like Burton. Do you think anyone will want a drink?" He held the bottle up.

"You're the host."

"Right." He reached for glasses. "There should be some ice."

"Willy is back. He must have sneaked out of the store."

"Hell." He peered out of the window.

"I was just going to call Peter."

"Poor cat. Another victim," Neil said, opening the freezer compartment of the fridge. "There's no ice." He extended the trays: the ice had evaporated. Or dried. Whatever ice did.

"I meant to make ice," Bron said, setting a plate of sandwiches on the table. "But I imagine they'll drink it without ice. I know I would."

She smiled at me and took the teapot into the living room.

Neil was silent as he poured drinks.

"Want one?"

"No, thanks. I'll keep Bron company in sobriety."

"I didn't put it out to tempt her," Neil said. "If that's what you're thinking. She's going to be tempted all the time. I'm just trying to be a good host."

"I wasn't thinking anything. I'd better take the cream and sugar in for the tea. And then I'll call Peter about that cat."

I looked out of the window. Willy was staring across the lawn at me.

The cat was still there when I left at five-thirty. He came running as soon as he saw me and wound himself around my ankles. I scooped him up and he nestled against my shoulder.

"You poor thing." Yellow cat eyes watched me. His paw reached out and touched my face. He purred and closed his eyes. He was just the right weight for my arms and there was something so trusting about him. And pathetic. I had never thought of cats being as loyal as dogs. His person was gone, a fact not comprehended by his little cat brain.

"Come on, then."

I settled him on the front seat of the car. He fell asleep.

I had never owned a cat. There was a scrawny black thing, half-wild, that used to hang around Gram's abandoned shed, but you hardly saw him, and one day he'd just disappeared. Also, a redneck down the road in Maine drowned a sack of kittens and I pulled the sodden bundle out of the pond, but the palm-sized creatures were dead. I bawled my eyes out and spent hours lining a shoe box with velvet for a coffin. There was Pumpkin, of course, and other friends had cats, and Marion's cat, Elmer, had died at the age of eighteen just before I met Peter. "I'll never have another cat," Marion had said, but I'd never thought of the pain behind that statement, or imagined her cradling grey Elmer (his photo showed just a cat) in her arms.

I wanted this cat.

I bought a cheap litter box and a bag of cat food on the way home.

"You poor, poor thing," I crooned, carrying Willy to the basement. We don't have a rec room because the ceiling in the cellar of our old Ontario cottage is too low, but a worn loveseat I was going to recover someday sat in the corner. I pulled a sheet out of the dryer, fluffed it into a nest and deposited Willy on it. "Just for a little while, boy. Then we'll see."

Willy purred.

The phone rang as Peter and Conrad arrived. It was hard to hear over Conrad's excited barking as Peter filled his dish (*Food! Food!*), but finally I understood that Suzanne Maloff, Burton's mother, was going to slit my throat for talking about her son on TV.

She was sending hit men; she had connections.

She would burn my house down.

Chapter Four

I should have called the police and had her charged with "uttering threats," but—

"Only a nut case," Peter said, watching Conrad gobbling his Technical Rice & Lamb. "She'll just deny saying it. Lowlife sleaze."

It took Conrad exactly one minute to swallow his food. The routine was that he would eat and then Peter would take him for his promenade. Conrad always darted for the back door where his red leash hung. Today he paused and sniffed at the basement door. But only for a moment, because Peter was attaching the leash.

After they left, I carried a saucer of milk to the basement. Willy hadn't moved; he was still curled into a ball on the sheet, but he stretched when he saw me and sniffed at the dish on my knee. "How about some milk, eh?" I set it on the floor. Willy stared at me, looked at the milk, then lifted a paw and touched my knee.

"You want me to hold the dish, is that it?"

He gazed impassively. For a second the end of his tail twitched. Didn't that mean he was cross? It seemed to me I had read somewhere that a waving cat tail meant anger. I drew my hand back. Willy extended a paw. No claws.

"Are you trying to tell me something?"

I lifted the milk. With a faint "meow," Willy lapped the milk from the dish on my knee.

What a cat.

Bron wasn't able to make the class.

"Juliana's still here," she sighed. "I've been helping her sort through Mrs. Maloff's clothes all day. I'd dearly love to get away but she wants to take us out for Chinese food."

I'd be able to go to the Walper Hotel after class, I thought.

The assignment had been to write about an incident connected to their childhood homes. For once, everyone had their work done, even Roberta, who wrote movingly about growing up on an apple farm in the Eastern Townships of Quebec. Brad, Marilyn Monroe forgotten, described Saturday afternoon in Scarborough— the adults drinking beer on the patio while he played Scrabble inside with his disapproving grandmother. Betsy Chalmers wrote about the apartment she and her mother had moved to after her father deserted the family. Saturday morning was tidy-up time— Betsy dusted and polished while her mother washed the kitchen floor and vacuumed. Then, her mother put on her "navy felt hat with the red feather" and Betsy wore her "green itchy wool coat" and the two of them took the streetcar to downtown Toronto, where they had tea at Simpsons.

Martha described visiting cousins in New York and Bella wrote about her brick house in Ottawa, where "the maple tree became an umbrella on hot and lazy summer days." One day a hobo came along, kidnapped them, and took the kids to a haunted house. Alas, "it was all a dream..." The children had fallen asleep under the tree.

Frederick wrote about his mother making jam and included recipes. Greg Theriault, who'd had his scalp almost shaved since the week before, related a story about playing hockey and dragging his poor father out of bed at six on winter mornings for practice.

Frances Harley's stern face softened as she read her story about piano recitals. "I still remember my blue dress with the white bow."

Amanda made a list, piling on detail after detail (the wicker sewing basket, the trivet painted with a duck). Nothing happened in her sketch, but the list gained momentum and there was an eerie sense as she ended with a description of her mother— dress, hair, posture, twisted wedding ring, the old-fashioned silver watch, the matted pink slippers— staring out of the window, her back to the home Amanda had so completely described.

Finishing, Amanda lowered her head. She had her hair scraped back into a bun, but the arrangement was slipping.

"Personal stories seem to have a richness that sheer invention doesn't have," I commented.

"But personal stories don't sell," Brad said, smiling his handsome smile. A discussion followed about the difference between the writing and the marketing. Betsy wondered if she could send her story to *Reader's Digest.* Roberta said her neighbour had encouraged her to submit her story to a magazine. Frederick thought a gourmet or cooking magazine might be interested in his piece.

"We'll spend a little time next week on submitting stories," I said, although few of their stories were ready to send anywhere.

Yes, Amanda said. She would love to go to the Walper Hotel with me.

"I really liked the way you just listed things," I told her when we were seated with our glasses of white wine and orders of garlic bread in a quiet corner of the Barristers' Lounge.

I enjoyed the ambience of the place— its dark wood, antique cabinets and solid chairs. The Walper was an old hotel, dating back to the late 1800s. The agreement to establish Ontario Hydro was signed there, and it was easy to imagine prosperous businessmen of ninety years before dining with their wives and waltzing in the Crystal Ballroom.

"Nothing happens," I went on, "but you know that something will happen. Something awful."

Amanda took a sip of wine and pinned up a loose strand of hair. "It's really about when my father died. A policeman came to the door. It was early evening and I was studying for a Latin exam. But I couldn't concentrate. Things seemed to— wave and shimmer. Dad wasn't supposed to be home. It was Friday and he worked until nine. Mom and I had eaten our macaroni and cheese. She had been pretty good lately. She had it in her head that she wanted a budgie, and Dad and I were going to buy one the next day, Saturday, for a surprise..."

"Do you think you can write it?"

"I don't know. But I'm going to try... All that talk about 'marketing' tonight," Amanda said. She grinned. "Maybe Brad will really have a bestseller," she mused.

We gossiped about the class for a while. I shouldn't have done so, but talking to Amanda felt like talking to an old friend. Briefly I considered saying that she didn't really belong in the class, that she should just write on her own, but I didn't know how she would take this. I hoped she didn't need the stimulus of a class in order to write.

"Bron wasn't there tonight," Amanda said.

"She has the sister of that woman who was killed staying with her."

"She's very quiet."

"She's gone through a bit of a hard time. She's trying to get on her feet and is staying with her ex-husband for now." I wasn't going to tell Amanda, even Amanda, about Bron's drinking problem. "Her ex is a good friend of ours. Bron and Neil hosted the wake. I went over there and got things organized while they were at the funeral."

"I saw on the news that the grandson's been arrested."

"His mother called me last night," I said, and went on to tell the story. Amanda was adamant that I should call the police. Women like Suzanne, she said, could be tough customers. She'd witnessed a fight between two prostitutes on King Street recently.

"I think she was drunk."

"She's probably drunk all the time. That's why you have to look out. Watch your back."

"What kind of connections could she have?" I shook my head.

"Bikers, thugs."

"I wish I hadn't opened my big mouth in that interview."

"What's done is done."

"She says Burton is innocent."

"She's his mother. Wouldn't he inherit if he was innocent? And then Mama gets her share. Or everything."

"The word 'Mama' doesn't suit her. Burton was taken away from her."

"Wonderful woman."

"I know."

"You should go to the cops."

"Our friend, Neil, is with the OPP."

"Really? You've got to be kidding."

"Why?" I realized Bron hadn't mentioned Neil in her stories— yet.

"Writers aren't supposed to have cops as friends!"

"You're being romantic. You're thinking of poets who wear torn jeans and black berets. I'm really the cookbook lady at heart."

It was after eleven when we parted outside the Walper.

"Sure you don't want me to accompany you to your car?"

Amanda was walking. It was chilly out and she had tucked her hair under a black cloche-type hat.

"Don't be silly."

"I'm going to walk you to the parking lot."

"You'll be protection against a biker for sure!"

"Come on. It's just a little out of my way. Indulge me or I'll lie awake all night worrying."

"You see," I said, getting into the Volvo, "safe from bikers and thugs. Want a drive home?"

"No thanks. It's only a few blocks. I need to clear my head after that wine or I won't be able to write tomorrow morning. Hey, come for lunch some time. At my place."

"I'd love to."

"And don't pick up any hitchhikers." Amanda tapped the hood and watched me drive away.

I had just passed Kitchener city limits when my car had a flat tire.

Chapter Five

Damn! If ever I could have used a cellular phone it was then. I'd thought of buying one, but the idea had always seemed silly.

To make matters worse, the batteries in the flashlight in the glove compartment were dead.

What now? After the city lights, the highway was dark and narrow. There was no moon and the flat was on the highway side. I turned the flashers on and sat. I had never changed a tire in my life. Driving would damage the rim. Without a light, I couldn't even see to make my way to a farmhouse to telephone the Canadian Automobile Association.

The Volvo could be rear-ended.

Some years ago, a young university student, Linda Shaw, had had her tires slashed at a restaurant stop on the way to London. Days later, searchers found her burned and mutilated body in a field.

I was wearing a dark coat. If I walked along the highway, I could be run over.

Eleven-thirty. I tried the flashlight again and checked that the doors were locked as a transport truck, followed by a Corvette, whizzed by.

The flat had to be Suzanne's work. She had followed me to the Walper and cut the tire while I was innocently drinking wine with Amanda.

But why hadn't Suzanne followed me here?

Because she'd grown bored waiting and gotten drunk.

A pick-up truck lumbered by.

Should I get out of the car? Move away from it?

I did have the flashers on.

If I was really late, would Peter call the cops? But I'd told him that I was probably going to the Walper Hotel.

Should I try to flag someone down?

Here it was again, the darkness I had glimpsed the night when Maria Maloff was killed.

It was nearly twelve-thirty before a police cruiser stopped. I started crying as soon as I saw the very young, earnest face of the constable.

"I think someone slit my tire!" I blubbered.

Had I been drinking?

"Only one glass of wine at the Walper Hotel. White wine with a student in my class... I teach creative writing and we went out for a drink, only one glass... I mean, I..."

The policeman shone his light (nice big flashlight) on the tire and asked for my license.

"You just relax now and I'll be right back."

He was. I wasn't a criminal, after all, and he wrote down my CAA membership number.

"CAA won't be long, this time of night. What makes you think someone slit your tire?"

It was too involved a story. I shrugged and suddenly realized how cold the night air was.

"We'll have your tire checked, Ma'am. I'll stay with you until the CAA truck gets here."

"Can you call my husband, too? He'll be worried."

But there was no answer at home. "I left a message on the machine," the officer said.

"He's probably out walking the dog."

"Kind of late for that, isn't it?"

"Conrad— our dog— always gets a walk this time of night, right before my husband goes to bed."

"I'd better get a statement about your tire," the cop said.

"I'm probably imagining things."

"You could have been killed, Ma'am."

And so, while we waited for CAA rescue, I told him about Suzanne Maloff's threatening phone call. He knew about Burton and I had a feeling he recognized Suzanne's name, although he didn't say.

"I feel stupid now," I said. "She was probably just drunk when she called me."

"That's no excuse. Some of these women do know some pretty bad characters. Take it from me. We'll investigate."

"She'll deny it."

He wrote in his notebook.

"I don't even know the woman," I said, as a tow-truck appeared. "I never met her."

The CAA driver decided to tow the Volvo into Guelph and change the tire there. It was one-thirty by the time I arrived at my front door.

Peter hugged me and said we should have called the police in the first place. He was in his pyjamas. I'd called him from the garage and he had a pot of tea waiting for me.

"Don't you notice something strange?" he asked, after I had shed a few more tears.

"What?"

"You really didn't notice anything different?"

"I've had enough 'different' for one night."

"No really!"

"What?"

"There's something wrong with the pooper. Didn't you miss him greeting you? He didn't even come to the door!"

Conrad was moping by the closed door to the basement. Sighing and looking sad and disgusted.

"I hope he doesn't have to throw up," Peter said. "I caught him crunching something when I had him off the leash. Do you think he ate a bone that's cut his intestines?"

"No," I said.

Chapter Six

It was impossible to say if my tire had been tampered with, I learned the next day. But the police were "continuing their investigation."

"It's all Mickey Mouse stuff as far as they're concerned," Peter sighed in The Bookworm. "Nothing will come of it."

His new assistant, Carrie Decker, had the flu, and I was helping unpack the fall books, which made me feel sad. I didn't have a new title out this year and it looked as if there wouldn't be another mystery for a while. I used to write every day, but suddenly the plots had dried up.

And, I thought, as I shelved a new Carol Shields novel, the class was re-awakening my old love, the short story. Amanda's work especially was an inspiration. I'd always meant to write about my childhood in Maine.

Maybe the writing retreat would help.

"I wish I hadn't mentioned Mrs. Maloff's death in that stupid interview," I said.

"If you're worried, take Conrad wherever you go."

Something suddenly occurred to me.

"That's why you've been keeping Conrad in the store! You *are* worried that horrible Suzanne will burn the house down!"

"He just seems not himself the past while," Peter said. "Moping around, not even wanting to go for a walk lately. I had to practically drag him outside last night."

Should I tell Peter about Willy? The cat had made himself at home in the basement, silently eating, sleeping and waiting for me to cuddle him. It was a silly secret to keep. Conrad was going to have to get used to the cat sooner or later.

"You don't really think that woman would try something?"

"Nah. People like her are all mouth," Peter said, and returned to checking invoices. I shelved books for a while and paused to dip into an anthology of stories by Norwegian women, which I put aside to take home.

"One of these days I'm going to write some more stories. Sometimes I think the computer's just programmed for mysteries."

"Write in the store," Peter suggested. "Maybe you need a change." His glasses had slipped down his nose. He didn't look up from the invoices.

"Maybe I do."

The thought of writing in the store was instantly appealing. I'd use a notebook, I decided, the way I used to do in my pre-computer days.

Yes, a wonderful notebook! I found just the thing at the Stone Road Mall: five hundred pages with inside pockets for clippings, random thoughts and inspiring quotations. The book had a nice, hard cover, protecting all that empty ruled paper.

Should I buy one or two? I used to buy a new notebook around New Year's, and although I never filled the pages, I loved knowing that journal was around.

Nine-ninety-five was a small price to pay for this renewed pleasure. I could hardly wait to begin.

I used to live in Maine, I wrote in a Tim Hortons doughnut shop, *beside the sea in a white house that my grandfather's father had built. But it was a woman's house. Great-grandfather died young and his widow, Emilia, raised five boys on her own. She did not want them to be fishermen. That was her prayer. Prayer! Two drowned at sea, consumption took another, and Edwin disappeared to Alaska, never to be heard from again. That left Grandfather, Albert, who married my grandmother, and as I write this I think that it was the men who became invisible.*

My father was invisible. Lesley Archer, who begot me and disappeared. Who was he? I knew not to ask in that white house beside the sea. My mother was absent, but not invisible. She was in Chicago... It was Grandmother who was always present.

There she is, standing on the back stoop, shaking out the tablecloth. Let me begin with that image. I am nine years old and shivering in my blue coat...

I was still writing when Neil came in.

"Saw your car." He slid into the opposite chair and eyed my notebook.

"Just scribbling away. I need a boost. Tim Hortons suddenly seemed to be the way to go. What're you doing? Playing hooky?"

Neil shrugged. There was a cut on his chin from shaving. He was wearing his old jean jacket with the worn collar.

"I felt kind of low this morning."

"Juliana still there?"

"Yeah. I have to drop stuff off at the Sally Ann."

"You need coffee, kiddo."

"What I need is something stronger," Neil said.

We went to the Albion, an old tavern in downtown Guelph. Neil ordered two draft.

"There are times," he sighed, "when not having beer in the house can be a drag."

"So you can drown your sorrows?"

"Yeah. Cheers." He took a big swallow and stared at the table. "Maybe I shouldn't have dragged you over here. I should wallow alone."

"What's going on? Juliana can't be that bad."

"She's okay."

"Enjoying the sorting, I bet."

We chatted a while about this and that. Neil kept running his hand through his reddish hair. Had something happened with Bron? Was she drinking again? Into the sherry with the robust Juliana? Girl talk at midnight, tears and recriminations?

What I learned, after Neil ordered a second beer, was worse. Much worse.

Chapter Seven

"Rape?" I stared at Neil. It wasn't possible. Not Neil. He was one of the kindest people I knew. He wasn't angry, or rigid, or... what? I didn't think I had ever known a rapist, but the word always reminded me of my ex, Charlie, with his verbal abuse and face contorted with rage. I had bad dreams about Charlie for years, and in some of these nightmares he would pin me to the bed and force himself into me. It was always a relief to wake up beside Peter.

No, I couldn't imagine Neil being a rapist.

The woman had worked in the OPP office in Leicester, where Neil was temporarily stationed six years ago. Her name was Helena Quintham, a heavy-set young woman with thick glasses. That was how Neil remembered her: just someone who'd passed through his life. "Helena

Quintham. The name meant nothing. I really had to think to recall her. She answered the phone and typed reports. Someone who worked in the office. She made the coffee and she'd bring it around, the way secretaries used to. The only time I was alone with her was when I gave her a lift to the garage so she could pick her car up. Something about the rear lights not working.

"I honestly don't know what she's talking about," Neil finished, draining his glass. He squeezed his eyes shut and shook his head. Except for a solitary man in the corner, gazing into space, we were the only customers in the Albion. I'd gone to poetry readings in this bar, but today the place seemed dreary, empty, unreal. Neil lowered his voice.

Helena claimed Neil had raped her during that car ride. Neil drove to the country, pulled onto a logging road and forced her to the back seat and raped her. He had called her a bitch, she said, and a lot of other names, and threatened to kill her if she told. She hadn't reported it. Two weeks later he cornered her in the office when she was working overtime and did it again.

("In the office!" Neil cried. "Anyone could have walked in.")

Helena quit her job, moved to Toronto and lived in terror that Neil would find her. She hadn't been able to have a normal relationship with a man, and had gone into therapy.

She suffered from bad dreams and couldn't hold a job.

She now felt she had no choice but to charge Neil with rape and to sue the OPP.

"It's a nightmare," Neil said.

"I don't believe it. I'd never believe it of you. Never, never. What happens now?"

"Internal investigation. They'll interview the Leicester staff. And it's gone to our legal people."

"They don't think you did it?"

"I don't know what to believe. There's a procedure we follow. It won't be hushed up. It can't be. I expect I'll be suspended with pay."

"Does Bron know?"

"Not yet. It's kind of hard with Juliana there."

"What're you going to do?"

"Tell the truth. Maybe some of the Leicester people will know something."

"Like this woman had a thing for you? Or disliked you for some reason. Maybe she's disturbed. Maybe she imagined it. You know, she had a dream and came to believe it was real." I thought of Charlie. "I don't see how anyone who knows you can possibly believe a thing like that! Your co-workers must believe you're innocent! What have they said so far?"

"They're supportive. At least they say they are. But they're taking this thing very seriously. Cops have done awful things."

"She hasn't actually charged you yet?"

"Not yet. But it'll come. It'll be in the papers, too. You wait and see."

"Maybe they'll remember you at that garage when you dropped this woman off."

"The place was closed. There was no one there. They'd forgotten she was supposed to pick her car up. I drove her home."

"Did you go inside? For a coffee?"

"Nope. I did not. I don't recall what I did the rest of the night, but I know it was the end of a shift. I probably went to the motel where I was staying."

"Did you eat in a restaurant?"

"I don't think so. I had a kitchenette. I probably nuked a TV dinner or something. It was just temporary. I usually came home to Guelph on my days off. Jane and I were still together for part of that year."

Jane was the woman he'd lived with in Guelph.

"Maybe Jane remembers something. Like, you told her you dropped this Helena person off."

"I wouldn't even know where to find her. She moved back to Toronto. She's married. But the legal people will talk to her."

"Did you part on bad terms?"

"Nah. After a while we just didn't click any more. Jane didn't like the cop business too much. I should get out of it, you know. If I clear my name, maybe I should quit the force."

"And do what?"

"Open a doughnut shop. A fishing-tackle place up north. Become a bum. Of course, if this thing sticks, I'll be staring at the bars of Kingston Pen."

"Don't say that!"

"It might happen, Carolyn. This is very serious business. Real bad trouble. That's why we always have a female police officer with us when we transport women. But I never imagined that something like this would happen with one of the staff."

"Aren't they vetted?"

"Sure they are. Helena obviously didn't have a criminal record. She attended the school she says she went to. She didn't take part in riots. She wasn't working to overthrow the government and no one in her family had been in serious trouble with the law. That kind of thing would be checked."

"What was she like?"

"Just a woman. I couldn't even picture her until they dug up a picture from an office party. She was holding a coffee, a styrofoam cup. An ordinary woman in a green dress. A bit overweight. And the glasses I did remember."

"Was she from Leicester?"

"I'm not sure. I never really got to know her. I kind of think she was from some country place."

"Were you still there when she left?"

"I couldn't say for sure, but I sort of remember signing a card. But maybe I was off."

"Maybe she felt slighted. Say she thought you cared for her and then you weren't even there to say goodbye. Maybe you were the love of her life, but you just saw her as a secretary."

"That's a hell of a way to show her love."

"People don't notice clerical staff. When I came to Guelph, I worked for a month or so as an office temp. You know, you sign up with an agency, and they get a cut of your pay. Men would call me 'the girl.' It wasn't much fun, but it was the norm back in the dark ages. 'I'll get my girl to call your girl.' That kind of thing."

"I don't think I ever called anyone 'a girl,'" Neil said.

"I'm just trying to make some sense of this. I know you didn't do it, Neil. The woman has to be crazy. Maybe she really believes it happened, like those people who think they were sexually abused as children and later recant."

"What it will come down to is my word against hers."

"Any jury would believe you!"

"That's where you're wrong. I'm the guy with the power. I'm the big policeman. I carry a gun; I can arrest people."

"And in small towns a cop would have a certain attraction." I thought of Bron. "At least once they would have. Or maybe it wasn't so long ago. Hugh was pretty influential in Meredith. Not with women, necessarily. But people listened to what he had to say. I bet he misses it today."

Neil drank his beer. His second. He had ordered two glasses of draft. He didn't say anything for a while. His life could be ruined, I realized, even if it went to trial and he was found not guilty. The suspicion would always be there that Neil had really done it.

"I wish I could talk to this Helena," I said.

"Don't even think of it," Neil said. "Her lawyer would love it."

"I feel awful," I said.

"They're giving me a lie detector test," Neil said. "On Monday. Ten in the morning."

I couldn't get over the fact that Neil could end up going to prison. A policeman wouldn't get very good treatment in the pen. Hardened criminals would make mincemeat of him. A rapist! I thought, driving home. Suddenly Steven's face came before my eyes. How was he faring? Allison said he worked in the prison library and he was taking correspondence courses, but it wasn't easy picturing him living with bank robbers and violent men. They would resent Steven's softness, his intelligence. And yet, he had committed a criminal act by posing as a doctor.

A car horn beeped. I had changed lanes without signalling. The driver raised her fist and stepped on the gas as she passed me to come to a screeching halt at the stop sign. A skinny blonde jumped out and headed toward my car. I rolled the window down.

"Who the hell do you think you are?" she screamed in my face. I could smell her strong perfume.

"I'm sorry. I was distracted. I just had some bad news. I..."

"You make me sick! 'I just had some bad news.' Hoity-toity, isn't she? Ever listen to yourself talk? Huh? You think you're wonderful, don't you?"

Her cheeks were flushed beneath her pancake make-up and her eyes were so thickly lined with kohl that it was hard to make out their colour.

"Step outside and let's get it over with!"

I started to roll up the window, but she was too quick for me. Before I knew what was happening she had a handful of my hair.

"Piece of slime! Garbage! That's what you are! Nothing but garbage!"

"Let go of me!"

"Like hell! You ain't seen nothing yet, lady! You just shut up because I got something to say to you! You're in one heap of trouble, I'll tell you that! Opening your big mouth! You think you're smart, don't you? Don'tcha? Huh?" She yanked harder, then let go. "I could kill you."

I couldn't drive away because her car, a long, green Chevy with a hanging muffler, rust spots and a Garfield in the back window, blocked mine. She yanked the driver's door open and tried to pull me out.

"Leave me alone. If you'll stop yelling, I'll get out. You are Suzanne, aren't you?"

"Shut up!"

She watched me climb out of the car. My scalp burned and my hands shook.

"Suzanne Maloff," I said, trying to keep my voice level.

She reached into the pocket of her black leather jacket and took out a package of du Maurier cigarettes. She had chains tattooed around both wrists.

"My scalp hurts," I said. "I don't really feel like talking to you."

"Well, don't then, Miss High and Mighty."

"You have a foul mouth," I said.

"At least it's not a big mouth, like yours!" She took a swing at me, grazing my chin. Her cigarette package fell to the ground. I crushed it with my foot. She thumped my arm. I hit her, hard, on her arm, and then we were on the ground.

The last fist fight I was in was when I was eleven years old, in Maine. A tough older girl, Angela, had, for some reason, taken a strong dislike to me. Angela nicknamed me "Minnie Tits" and followed me around the schoolyard chanting this. Soon she was joined by her friends, younger girls who did her bidding, who scratched and pulled my hair. One day I had had enough and ploughed my head into Angela's puffy stomach. That sent her to the ground and I bit her through the arm of her winter coat.

"Bitch, you bitch!" Suzanne said.

"Minnie Tits!"

That stopped her. "Bitch," she said one more time, but she sat up and looked at her chest. She wore a tight, striped top, but she didn't have big breasts.

"Have a smoke," I said, retrieving the package and tossing it to her. There was a bruise on her chin. I looked around, but no one was watching. A car swerved around our parked vehicles.

"I should call the police," I said.

"Yeah, you're good at that. I didn't make any damn phone calls to you. I've got enough on my plate. I never threatened you." She sat down on the strip of grass beside the sidewalk.

I remained standing.

"Sure you did. You threatened me today."

"I had every right to threaten you! You're lucky I didn't take up my threats."

"Tough, aren't you?"

"I got enough on my plate without getting accused of something I didn't do."

"You didn't even call me the day I was on TV? And hang up?"

"Nope." She looked away, though, and I was sure she was lying. "Like I've got nothing better to do than waste my time fooling around on the goddamn phone. Sure. My kid gets charged with murdering that old bitch and I spend my time playing telephone. Sure. I never threatened you on the damn phone!"

She looked right at me. So she had called and hung up, but she hadn't threatened to burn my house down and so on.

"You gonna call the cops?" The cigarette smoked between her fingers.

"Why shouldn't I?"

She shrugged.

"Because you've been in trouble before and you'll be in a helluva lot more trouble if I call, right?"

"Sounds like someone's been talking to you and guess who that is, eh? Pretty good buddies with that cop next to the old lady's place. And Burton didn't kill her. Just 'cause he was in trouble once don't mean he killed her."

"How do you know he didn't kill her?"

"He's my kid. I know my kid. But he'll serve time, that's for sure. They'll get him for it and throw away the key. Even his lawyer wants him to plead temporary insanity. That's what you get with a greenback lawyer from legal aid. Burton's just pissed off enough to go for it."

"If he's innocent, he should stick to his story."

"What the hell do you know?"

"Not much."

"Burton didn't do it 'cause he was at my place. They don't believe me. Cops all stick together."

Her head was bowed and her hair hung down, hiding her face. The bleached hair resembled straw and the roots were black.

"The next time you phone me, don't hang up," I said.

She was still sitting on the ground, smoking morosely, as I manoeuvred the Volvo around her car.

My scalp smarted.

"You mean you were rolling around on the ground?" Mark asked the next day after we had taken the dogs for a run. "Like fishwives fighting? I can imagine the headlines. Local Author in Confrontation with Hooker."

He laughed and ran his hands through his hair. It was shot through with grey now, but he still had that Bob Dylan look he had always cultivated.

"She's a stripper, not a hooker," Emma said. "There's a difference. And it's not funny."

"Exotic dancer," Peter said. But he didn't think it was so funny, either. He wanted me to call the police. People just weren't supposed to go around hitting each other, he'd said. "Call her an exotic dancer."

"She's exotic, all right." Mark knew her— or rather, knew of her. He'd been in court when Suzanne was charged with illicit lap dancing. All the legal people in Guelph knew her, it seemed. The police, too. I wished I felt okay about calling Neil, but he had enough, as Suzanne might have said, "on his plate."

I had told only Peter about Neil's trouble.

"I haven't seen her for years," Mark said. "Is she still a bottle blonde? With dark roots?"

"Weren't you observant?" Emma mused.

"I've never even seen a stripper," Peter said. "I mean with her clothes off. There was a girl, Wanda, in Meredith, who supposedly took to stripping after she moved to Toronto. She left school in grade nine. That's what everyone claimed. I couldn't see it myself. 'Stinky Wanda' we called her."

"They look different under the bright lights," Mark said. "Especially when you're young and drunk. We used to go to the old Coronet in Kitchener when I was a kid. We had phoney IDs. It was a big deal. None of us had ever had a girlfriend. It was *Playboy* all the way."

"There wasn't any *Playboy* on the farm," Emma said, referring to the commune.

"Too bourgeois," Mark laughed.

We bantered a while. Peter said his mother had found his *Playboy*. "Even nerds had *Playboy*," Peter admitted.

"I'm sure Thomas has never read the thing," Emma said.

"My mother probably said the same thing," Peter told her.

"My mother pretended not to see," Mark put in. Mrs. Richman was a real snob. "It could be right in front of her eyes and she'd say she never saw it."

"Suzanne's not the only one to stick up for her kid," I said. "Maybe she's making the alibi up, but I can understand it."

"What a bind to be in," Emma said. "I feel for her. Any mother would act crazy if her kid might go to prison. Especially for something he didn't do. I know how I'd feel if Thomas got in trouble."

"Luckily there's a lawyer in the family," Mark said. He patted Emma's shoulder on his way to get milk out of the fridge. Emma's eyes followed him. A few years ago, Mark wouldn't have made that statement. Things really did seem to be looking up for them, I thought, as Emma set the teapot and a plate of honey cake on the pine table in the dining area of their sunny kitchen. A new quilt hung over the table— a magical scene of children skating on a country lake in which Emma had incorporated pieces of bark and bits of stone.

"Where is Thomas today?" I asked, as Emma poured tea.

"Out with his love, Patricia," Mark said. "So you want me to find out about Burton?"

"You're reading my mind."

"She's just a softie," Peter said. "Doesn't he already have a lawyer?"

"Legal aid," I said. "His mother wasn't impressed."

"You'd be surprised." Mark said. "Some of those legal aid people are terrific. Young mavericks out to make a name for themselves. But I can ask around. The police must have had some real evidence to charge the guy."

"You know they've arrested wrong people in the past. People who've served long years. Sometimes they just want to arrest someone. I'm not saying that Burton didn't do it, but his mother was like a madwoman about it. What if she's telling the truth, but no one will believe her because of who she is?"

"I would lie for Thomas," Emma said.

"Even if he killed someone?" Peter asked.

Emma said, "Thomas would never kill anyone."

Chapter Eight

It was selfish, considering Neil's trouble, but it felt wonderful to get to work in The Bookworm. The solace of that notebook! It recalled the long-ago days when I buried myself in paper and pen. Charlie might scoff and sneer, saying I would never amount to anything, but the pages were always there for me. Didn't Anne Frank say that paper was patient?

Peter suggested clearing out the storage room for my writing space, but after we wrestled boxes of used paperbacks to the basement and moved in a display table, I found the small room with its single light bulb claustrophobic and spent the rest of the morning straightening shelves and keeping Peter company. "I'd go back to the doughnut shop," I told Peter, "but I'd never get any sleep after all that coffee. There's really no reason I can't write at home."

"You can't because you can't," Peter said, as he prepared the bank deposit. "Maybe you need distractions, like doughnuts and books."

"I'd always be reading, here."

But after he left (taking Conrad, who was spending all his days at the store lately; he was so antsy at home; what was I going to do about the cat?), I drifted to the corner armchair where browsers could be comfortable.

The girl has falling-down white knee socks and black, scuffed Mary Janes. There is a bandaid on one knee, just visible beneath the blue wool coat with its darker velvet collar. She is wearing her very best pink party dress, and she is holding Teddy. Mom wanted to throw Teddy out— Teddy was dirty and torn and what would Gram say? But the girl cried and screamed and Mom said, "Have it your way! You always do!"

Now the girl stands in Gram's front room clutching the toy. A button has come off her coat and Mom is fussing. Gram says, "It's all right, Shirley."

The girl tries not to cry. She is small, not pretty, with a pointy face. Her curly hair would be pretty if it were bright, but it's brown, like brown mice, unlike Mom's yellow hair which is shiny like the moon, like gold.

It is cold in the front room because Gram did not know they were coming. There are teacups and princess figurines in a glass case and there is a glass globe on a stand by the window. The globe contains a ship from olden times.

Gram says, "Come into the kitchen, for heaven's sake."

A mystery: why are they in the front room? It is late fall and the special room has to be heated, unlike the kitchen with its big stove and smell of wood.

Has the girl been here before? Does she remember the field that stretches to the sea, the green swing beside the lilac bushes, the upturned dory? Later, the girl will remember nothing from before except a room with green wallpaper and a streetcar.

"It's only for a little while," Shirley says. "Until I get things settled.

"I have everything packed and cleaned," she adds, indicating the brown suitcase. "All her things."

Inside the suitcase: small white underpants, striped pyjamas with red roses on them, the blue and red dungarees for play, stained white blouses with pearl buttons, red slippers from Santa, a navy skirt the girl has outgrown, and a mauve dress with a torn lace collar. Toothbrush, two Golden Books— Hansel and Gretel *and* Goldilocks and the Three Bears*, a string of plastic beads.*

Gramps is there, tugging at his cap. They go to the warm kitchen where the window shows a weathered shed. Everything is grey, foggy, damp, sea-salt wet.

Gramps is small, Gram big with an apron over her front. Gramps gives the girl a quarter.

No, the girl won't remove her coat after Shirley leaves. She elbows Gram away, stamps her feet and clutches Teddy.

And later, when the memories stretch to goodness, to cocoa on winter evenings and games of Crazy Eights and running through the field to the place where Gramps keeps his big boat, that day in the cold front room where Shirley paced, anxious to be gone (for a drink, a man, a good time), remains, strangely, not of this seaside place but of somewhere else, somewhere in-between where she has never returned.

The girl is me...

I didn't touch the class assignments until late Wednesday evening, and the class, this time, seemed an annoying interruption.

"No drinks at the Walper tonight, I'm afraid," I told Amanda after class. "I was really looking forward to it, but I have to get back to Guelph."

I had to drive Bron home.

"I really wanted to talk to you, too," Amanda said. "Why don't we get together next week? Do you want to come for lunch one day? You could come to my place."

We decided on one o'clock the next Monday.

Bron knew about "Neil's predicament" as she called it. "It's all nonsense, an idea a crazy woman has, but I have a terrible feeling that this thing isn't going to end well," she said on the way home. "And Juliana is there and that makes it awkward, too."

"Has he told Juliana?"

"No. He says he'll tell her before she leaves so she won't find out from the newspapers. But she knows something is wrong. The atmosphere at home is something else! I had to get out tonight. Neil sits brooding in front of the TV and won't talk, which isn't like him. They're going to suspend him before it becomes public."

"Do you think he'll quit the force?"

"He's talking about it. If only he'd done it years ago! It wasn't a picnic, by any means. Shiftwork and the ever-present danger and what was really bad was when he went undercover in Toronto. Maureen and I had to stay behind in this small town near London where I didn't know anyone other than OPP wives while Neil hung around looking like a druggie on Yonge Street. We had just moved and they put Neil on the street. Even the Metro police didn't know he was undercover. He was mixing with the scum of the earth and when he came home a day a week he wasn't himself. To tell you the truth, I think he was scared. He'd go boozing with his cop buddies but he wouldn't talk to me about what was worrying him. We were at each other's throats all the time. And sometimes he didn't come home.

"Maureen would cry when her dad didn't come home. She hasn't had it easy, either."

"Does Maureen know?" I had never met Neil and Bron's daughter.

"Neil can't bring himself to tell her. He wants me to give her the bad news. I'm supposed to go to Toronto to see her. But how can I go while Juliana's still there?"

"Maybe you shouldn't wait," I said. "You could tell Juliana you had a doctor's appointment or something."

"I think Neil should tell her," Bron said, shifting her purse. "But maybe it's too hard for him. Maureen works with rape victims. She's always saying women aren't believed. I have no idea how she'll react. She's heard all these stories about supposedly nice men who rape women on dates or who hide behind the bushes. This is going to crush her."

"You should go to Toronto soon. The sooner the better. I'll even drive you."

"I was going to take the train."

"You don't have to take the train. It'd be another nuisance. I'll drop you off at Maureen's and go to see my publisher, do a bit of shopping. I haven't been to Toronto for a while. Let me know when you want to go."

"Maureen works and I don't want to tell her in front of her husband. It's better she learn it on her own. I'd have to see her on her lunch hour or after work."

"What's wrong with her husband?"

"Bruce doesn't like the police. That's putting it mildly. He thinks cops are nothing but hooligans. He and Neil are polite, but Neil prefers not to acknowledge the bad feelings. He sees but doesn't see."

"How does Maureen feel about her father being with the OPP?"

"She thinks he's the exception to the rule. She sticks up for her father with Bruce, but I don't know how the rape charge will affect that. Bruce likes to think of himself as real gentle, a tree-hugger, but there's a conservative streak in him. Holier than thou. I don't think he likes me either. Because of— you know— my old problem. Bruce comes from a prominent Muskoka family. The tennis crowd. I think he feels Neil and I are common, especially after I got drunk at their wedding reception, which was held on his father's damned houseboat. I almost fell into the lake."

"Well, I'll drive you to Toronto. Just say when."

There goes a day of writing, I told myself.

I wasn't at home for ten minutes when Bron phoned. Maureen had a cancelled appointment the next day and could see her mother at eleven.

Chapter Nine

Maureen worked at the Carr Women's Centre. It was on one of the old downtown streets, a three-storey building shaded by a big maple tree. A gaunt woman sat smoking on the outside stairs.

"You can't smoke in there," Bron sighed. She had been chain-smoking since Guelph. "I'll have to bite my nails instead. You sure you don't want to come in with me?"

"I'd like to meet Maureen, but I think this isn't the time. I'll be back at one-thirty."

"And if things go wrong, I'll go to the Eaton Centre, meet you in the food court. I'm not sticking around if Maureen says she doesn't believe her father."

I decided not to go to see my publisher, Jake Hendricks, who had been hinting about the next mystery. He felt inspiration would come to me one starry night, and bingo, I'd have the next book for him.

Instead, I lost myself for a few hours in the Eaton Centre, where I mingled with the shoppers. Today, the three floors of shops seemed to be filled with well-dressed, middle-aged women, real Toronto matrons in beige all-weather coats accented by expensive purses. Olde Canada.

They were oddly reassuring and I drifted with them, buying postcards in the Museum Store and a reduced-price book by May Sarton at Coles. Did I need new shoes? Yes, yes; the chunky black lace-ups immediately cheered me, and why not get a long rayon dress to go with them? I bought Hallowe'en trinkets for Timmy and Jody and found a computer game for Matthew.

I treated myself to a cappuccino and a slice of white chocolate torte. In a couple of hours I had blown a month's teaching stipend.

I had to circle the block a few times before I found a parking spot near the Carr Centre. Bron sat on the steps. She had been crying.

"Maureen has taken the rest of the day off." Bron ground out her cigarette as she stood up. "Do you mind if we get out of here? Right now?"

It was awful, Bron said. Maureen cried and cried and kept asking, "How can they do this?" Everyone heard her and Bron suggested they go for a walk but Maureen insisted on calling Bruce at his law office. Bruce had an appointment he couldn't cancel, but he was coming home right after that. Maureen was afraid Bruce would want to confront Neil. What would Bruce's parents say? And how about his law partners?

"She wanted to know who the woman was," Bron said, "and she was furious when I wouldn't give her Helena's name. I promised Neil. He doesn't trust Bruce. I know they'll call Neil and try to find out."

She lit another cigarette.

"I know Bruce will say that Neil's guilty. He'll try to convince Maureen."

"I could drive you to Maureen's," I said. We weren't out of the city yet.

"I can't face Bruce today. I know I should be there, but I can't. I really can't. Call me a coward. And Maureen doesn't want me to hear what Bruce has to say. And how will Maureen square this thing with her co-workers? Who will all take Helena's side."

The day in Toronto interrupted my writing. Interrupted? The notebook was suddenly superfluous, childish scribbling. I slept in until eleven on Saturday and woke up to find Willy scratching at the basement door.

"You want to see the rest of your home, do you, little guy?"

I stood aside but he sat, unmoving, on the top step.

"Come on, then."

He didn't blink. I scooped him up and carried him to the living room. He stiffened in my arms and his ears went flat as I set him on the couch, which was covered with a red quilt because of Conrad's hair. "It's all right, the big dog's at the store with Peter."

I stroked his back and his chin, but he jumped off and crouched beneath the table where I kept current reading and the assignments from the class. Everything was dusty, even the pile of books. I hadn't dusted or vacuumed all week and the woven blue and white rug was covered with yellow dog hair. I could have written my initials in the dust that coated the pine furniture.

Willy jumped across the room and hid behind the bookshelves. I couldn't coax him out and couldn't reach him without moving the bookcase, which would mean removing all the books.

It would be mayhem, lamps and tables knocked over, if Conrad came home and found Willy, the source of the cat scent he'd been smelling all week.

"Come on, baby." I squeezed my hand into the space between the wall and the back of the shelving, but I couldn't reach him. His yellow eyes glowed.

Not even a saucer of milk tempted him.

There is nothing like cleaning to clear the mind. A lot of the writers' books advised women writers to forget the dust and get to work, but I always had to straighten up before I could begin. Maybe if you had "a room of your own" it would be different, but my study was attached to the eating area in the large addition we had put onto our small stone house. That work space was wonderful when I wrote the cookbooks.

Pottery jars of dried flowers and hanging copper pots were exactly the right inspiration. Cozy, cozy. The atmosphere had even helped the mysteries: security and comfort and familiarity while I wrote about murder and violence.

I washed the kitchen floor, went outside and picked apples from the tree in the back yard and baked three apple pies.

Willy came out as I slid the pies into the oven.

What was really on my mind as I did housework was, of course, Neil. The whole thing was so unfair, so improbable... but what if he was... guilty? Not of rape, but of something. The thought took me by surprise, but as soon as it entered my head I knew it had been hovering.

What if— *what if*— he had somehow gotten involved with the woman? Neil was sympathetic, warm, easy to talk to. He could have smiled in that way of his when that woman— Helena— served him his coffee. He was older than the young bucks who didn't even remember her name. She had never had a boyfriend. She was always the girl who sat by the phone, waiting. The girl no one asked for a dance at high school proms. The girl who went the extra mile— like delivering the coffee— but it didn't matter... A chubby, small-town girl... Clapboard house, elderly parents? Painting her face, wearing "in" (but cheap) clothing made things worse. People laughed. She felt like a fraud.

A friendly word, a chat by the roadside, tears welling behind her thick glasses. She had dreamed of Neil, fantasized about him. He was divorced, and if he was living with a woman, that wasn't marriage.

She would do more for him than bring him his coffee (just the way he liked it; had he noticed?). She would cook, and comfort him. She understood about the hours he had to work, his worries— unlike the woman he lived with. Neil would have mentioned Jane. "Late again. She wanted to see a movie tonight."

There would have been hope for her in that car that evening. "Don't worry. I'll drive you home," Neil would have said, patting her shoulder.

"You are a worry wart, aren't you?" It was wonderful for her, but she cried. She didn't want him to feel sorry for her. Or did she?

"Is something bothering you?"

She would have thick knees, heavy calves rising above boots that were too tight on her legs. Polyester skirt riding up. But in that dark car, in the shut-down town, they might have been the only people in the world. Neil hugged her...

Helena would turn this memory over and over in her mind, convinced that Neil wouldn't admit his true feelings.

He had a disease, cancer. He had only months to live, and he didn't want to burden her. If she could only get him alone, she would tell him it didn't matter. She knew, *knew* that if only they were alone he would be loving.

That was the important thing, to be alone with him again. She didn't expect him to take her to a movie or to dinner, to meet her parents, to introduce her to his friends. Being alone with him was all that mattered, to have his love again.

It took weeks, a month, and then it happened. She stayed to do the filing, Neil was in his office writing reports. She saw at once when she stood in the doorway that he did not love her. It was in his eyes. They turned away. He didn't reach out his arms. "You're working late, aren't you?" His tone would be brusque, off-hand.

But no! It wasn't supposed to be this way! she thought, staring at the back of his neck when he turned away. The hair that grew, like down, touching his collar. His strong shoulders... How lonely he looked! How apart!

"I was waiting for you."

A picture was forming. A girl at university, Janice. A formless face, small eyes, thick hips. Terribly bright at math. She did assignments for boys, bought them coffee, returned their books to the library. She followed a succession of guys around, but she became fixated, finally, on Malcolm MacGibbon, a Kennedy look-alike, and sent him love letters, Valentines, called him up, and trailed after him when he went on dates.

Everyone was shocked when Janice became pregnant with Malclom's child.

People blamed her.

Would Neil lie to me?

"It was awful," Bron whispered into her bedroom phone Sunday night. "I don't know what to do. I haven't seen Neil this angry for years. Bruce started as soon as they arrived. No more Mr. Nice Guy. It was like Bruce was the police, not Neil. You should have heard him. Bruce kept saying, 'There must be something you've forgotten. Someone doesn't make an accusation like this out of the blue!'"

"What about Maureen?"

"She kept crying, saying, 'We know you're innocent, Dad,' and then Bruce told her to be quiet. Neil pretty well threw Bruce out. Bruce looked at Maureen and told her to make up her mind. Come or stay. She went with her husband. I think that's what bothers Neil the most. She just trotted away behind that prick."

"Maybe he's abusive."

"I've always had my suspicions. Not of physical abuse, but he's so controlling. There she is, counselling women, and she needs help herself."

"What did you do?"

"I told Maureen we were there for her. I kissed her goodbye. And I gave Bruce a piece of my mind, which will make everything worse. I didn't think things could get worse, but they did. Poor Juliana stayed in the basement, hiding out. She's leaving tomorrow."

"That's one good thing."

"I'm not so sure. At least with her here, Neil can't go entirely to pieces. He's been drinking. I can smell it. He's got a bottle in his room."

"Oh, Bron."

"Don't worry. I haven't fallen off the wagon yet, but I sure am tempted. It's good having you to talk to."

"I'm always here," I said.

"Everything is going to get a lot worse. I know it," Bron said.

Chapter Ten

It felt good to go to Amanda's— to forget about Neil for a few hours.

Her place was exactly the way I had pictured it: an apartment in one of the large brick houses downtown near the library, on a tree-shaded street. Prosperous German merchants had built these homes when the city was still called Berlin. The name change to Kitchener during World War One had caused much dissension. There were brawls in the street and the Kaiser's bust was torn from its pedestal in Victoria Park and tossed into the lake.

Amanda threw open the door with its stained glass window and ushered me into the yesterday-today's artsy mélange she had created in her first-floor flat. An upright piano, ornately carved ("My mother's. She hadn't played in years. Don't ask me why I kept it."), covered with pottery and a large wicker figure of a woman, faced a wall of bright books on pine shelves. The sofa was a fifties' green monstrosity, draped with a red shawl. Plants hung over the Victorian love seat in the bay window. Her computer sat on a modern desk, but next to it was a red trunk adorned with a vase of autumn leaves. Framed Degas posters alternated with modern art posters.

"It's lovely," I told her as she took my coat.

"Mother would die if she saw her things mixed with my mish-mash." She wore a blue apron and her hands were floury. She held my coat by her fingertips. "I had to get rid of oodles of stuff, but I dragged a lot of it with me. Like the piano. There's this pantry type of thing, where I've got the extra junk stashed. Come into the kitchen while I finish the quiche."

"You shouldn't have gone to so much trouble."

"It was going to be President's Choice but I woke up this morning feeling energetic."

I sipped white wine while she mixed eggs. The kitchen was in its original state, with high counters and a huge sink, but Amanda had brightened it up with trailing spider plants and a copy of Van Gogh's "Sunflowers."

"I just love these old Kitchener houses," I said.

"Me, too. It's hell to heat and the windows are draughty, but I didn't want to go into one of the highrises. My father's family lived not far from here. Their place wasn't so large— no stained glass or anything like that— just a good Kitchener house, paid for in hard-earned dollars." She poured the eggs into the pie crust and took a sip of her wine.

"This place makes you feel connected," I mused.

"Yeah. Sometimes I think of the Christmases they must have had here, the kids coming home rosy-cheeked after skating in Victoria Park. It was probably a pretty dull life, all told, but over time it acquires charm. At least for me. Come on, I'll show you around."

She had brought her mother's dining room suite from Toronto. The heavy dark wood pieces filled the back room which overlooked a small garden where pumpkins grew on their vines and a striped deck chair stood on a patch of grass.

"How could I go into a modern apartment with this stuff?" Amanda straightened the woven blue placemats. The table was set with yellow goblets and white china dishes rimmed in gold. "I don't know what I was thinking of. Having dinner parties, maybe. Hah! Maybe I thought I'd meet a good and solid burgher and play long-ago."

She had chosen the smallest room for her bedroom. The double bed, covered with a quilt, took up almost all the floor space. There were more books in a wicker shelf which also served as a night table and I noticed a stack on the floor. *Accordian Crimes*, *Not Wanted on the Voyage*, Dylan Thomas's *Quite Early One Morning* and several mysteries and true crime books. Amanda pushed the latter under the bed. "You weren't supposed to notice the junk," she laughed.

"We can't be high-brow all the time."

"Indeed we can't."

"I have some of your mysteries. You can autograph them for me. And they're not under the bed. They have their respectful places on the shelf."

It was an enjoyable lunch. I told her about my notebook writing, about Willy the cat. I dramatized the story of Suzanne "punching me out" and we talked about fights we'd had as kids (Amanda had given a girl a black eye because the girl had tried to lift her skirt to show the boys in the school playground Amanda's underwear); about food and houses, which, we agreed, women invariably talked about.

"Suzanne sounds dangerous to me," Amanda said, serving the coffee.

"I sure wasn't expecting her to beat me up. What if someone had seen?"

"Then they would have called the police," Amanda said.

I wished I could discuss Neil's problems with her, and when Amanda told me that she had bought the white china in preparation for the marriage-that-never-was, I let the conversation drift to Bron, who led to Neil. I explained how Neil and I had met after my mother-in-law and I discovered the body of a man we had wanted to talk to. The only other policeman I had ever known was my father-in-law, I told Amanda. Neil wasn't like "a cop" at all, I said, and spoke of his kindness to Mrs. Maloff's sister.

"He sounds like a nice guy. Bron's nice, too. I like her stories. It was good of them to put the sister up."

"Neil's from out west. He says westerners are hospitable. He's even driving the sister to the airport tomorrow. She's from the west, too. Neil was a minister's son. The last thing his parents wanted was for him to become a policeman."

"Isn't that always the way? Dad never wanted me to work in offices, either, but I went through a time where I wanted to quit school and sell make-up at Eaton's. Poor Dad. We had one of our few rows over that one. Kids can be so stupid. I dyed my hair blonde and even failed a Latin exam. But I got over that nonsense. I didn't like the dumb kids I was hanging around with. Especially this one guy who wanted to marry me. He robbed a corner store and that was that.

"More coffee? There's a bit of wine left, too."

"Coffee's fine."

"Have you noticed I don't have photos displayed?"

"Now that you mention it..."

"I found I couldn't write with them starting at me. Macabre, isn't it?"

"I can understand that."

"Anyway, let me show you. You've heard enough about them in my stories."

With what myths we imbue the ordinary, I thought, staring at a silver-framed picture of a balding man in a suit. He looked shy, kind, with a broad face and steel-rimmed glasses. It had been taken when he was appointed general manager of his department, Amanda said.

The mother was posed at the CNE, sitting in a wicker chair. She wore a sun hat and smiled tentatively. She was a moderately pretty woman with sandy hair who would not have stood out in a crowd in her flowered summer dress. No frothing maniac, and if I hadn't known her story, I would have put her down as a suburban housewife who was perhaps a little retiring.

"It was just before Dad's heart attack," Amanda said. "Here's their wedding picture."

The young Mr. and Mrs. Gray were solemn, she in a slender, trailing white gown, he in a dark suit. She carried a bouquet; he held a top hat. The photo had yellowed. It could have been taken at the turn of the century instead of in 1950. The couple looked old-fashioned with none of the gaiety you saw in wedding photos today. He was clerking in a bank; she would stay at home. No matter what, they would never divorce.

"I rarely look at them any more," Amanda said, replacing the pictures in a desk drawer. "Not only do the pictures keep me from writing, but they distort the reality I have in my head. But I've thought of using the photos in the book. The way Carol Shields did in *The Stone Diaries*, although the story wasn't about her family."

"It's an interesting idea."

"Once I finish the stories I'll put them together with some photos, maybe get the pictures scanned and see how the whole thing looks."

At the door, Amanda said, "I'm so glad I signed up for your class. I wasn't going to, you know. I thought it would be trite and I'd feel... I don't know. Silly. I guess I didn't want my writing exposed yet. And now I'm even going on a retreat with the famous Carolyn Archer!"

"But you turned into my star pupil," I said. "And a friend," I added.

Chapter Eleven

Mark came into The Bookworm and interrupted my writing just as I was getting into a story about visiting my mother in Chicago.

"Sorry I haven't called." He looked at my notebook. He was wearing his lawyer outfit today, a grey suit. "What are you doing, taking inventory?"

"Just scribbling. I thought I'd try writing in the store."

"That's a new one, isn't it?" He shrugged and didn't wait for an answer. In the commune days, Mark had had aspirations to write song lyrics, but nothing came of them and perhaps that was why he never talked much about my writing. "Let's go grab a coffee and I'll fill you in."

Would he let me take him away from a court case? I wondered crossly, but I put my notebook away.

There was little point in believing Burton was innocent, he told me over coffee; Burton wouldn't admit to shooting his grandmother, but he had confessed to hitting her and knocking her to the ground.

"You haven't heard from the mother, I take it? No more brawls in the mud?"

"No more brawls in the mud."

"She's a real character. Stay away from her. She's been up on assault charges before— tavern fights and the like. She bashed another stripper with a beer bottle and put the girl out of commission for a while. Lovely woman."

"Hey, maybe she did in the grandmother, and Burton's protecting her," I mused. "Especially as they're each other's alibis. Maybe she shot Granny because Granny wouldn't give Burton money. Money that would filter down to her. Or she shot her because of past grievances. The old people hated her."

"I wouldn't waste my time on this if I were you. And stay away from that Suzanne. If she bothers you again, call the cops. Have you heard about your friend Neil?"

"What?"

"The rape thing. Don't tell me you don't know. Of course you know. Word is it's going to come out any day. I don't envy him. What a predicament to be in. Even if he's innocent— "

"—of course he's innocent."

"It'll be his word against hers. And if he gets off, it'll always hang over his head. It'll ruin his career."

"I'm surprised you know about it. Who told you?"

"Someone I went to school with who's in the Attorney-General's office. Don't repeat this."

"What'll happen now?"

"Neil will be charged. He'll be suspended with pay for the time being. I'm telling you, Carolyn, it's going to be awful. All the rape victims' groups will be up in arms; there'll be talk about police brutality. You name it. You know what happens."

"You couldn't ask for a nicer guy than Neil. He would never rape anyone."

"Try telling a jury that," Mark said. "The woman's doctor will testify. Her friends will talk about her suffering, her emotional trauma. I wouldn't want to be in his shoes."

"You talk like Neil doesn't have a chance."

"Sure he has a chance. But it'll be hell. In the meantime, he and his family will go through agony. Things will never be the same for him again."

How could I go back to my notebook after that? It was 12:30 and I busied myself straightening books. I ate my cheese and alfalfa sprout sandwich and then it was almost two. The store was busy and I waited on customers.

I left at four, and stopped at the IGA, where I bought a chicken. I was slicing garlic when Bron called.

"Neil's not back yet. Juliana's plane left at ten. He said he'd drive straight home."

"Maybe the plane was delayed."

"It wasn't. I checked."

"He could have run into a friend and gone for a beer."

"He's too worried and uptight to do that. Maureen hasn't seen him, either. She's still off work. She hung up on me. Do you think Neil's done something foolish?"

"Like what?" I didn't want to say that Neil might have found out about the charges being announced soon.

"I don't want to say it. You have no idea how down he is. And the argument with Bruce and Maureen made things so much worse. Do you know what he said last night? 'What's the point of going on?' I've never seen him so low."

"Maybe he went to see a lawyer."

"He's already seen the OPP legal people. Why isn't he back? I think I'm going crazy."

"Do you want to come here?"

"I have to stay here in case Neil calls."

"I'm sure he'll be home soon."

"He's not responsible to me but he knows I'd be worried. I even wish Juliana was still here so I'd have someone to talk to."

"If Neil isn't back after we eat, I'll come over," I told her.

Neil didn't come home. Later, Peter stacked the dishwasher while I "put some laundry in downstairs." Poor Willy meowed plaintively as soon as he saw me and watched while I cleaned the litter box in its hiding place behind the furnace. For the first time, he sat on my lap and purred while I stroked him.

"One of these days you'll live upstairs," I told him, avoiding his sad eyes when I left.

I put on a clean sweatshirt and jeans so Bron wouldn't have an allergic reaction to the cat dander, but her eyes were already red when Peter and I arrived. There was cigarette ash on her blue sweatshirt.

"I have a terrible feeling," Bron said. "Something's not right."

The ashtray was overflowing and the sink was filled with empty coffee mugs.

"Neil definitely planned to come right home," she repeated. "He didn't want to see anyone. He almost called a limo to deliver Juliana to the airport. I wish he had."

For two hours we went over and over what could have happened to Neil. Circles and circles. Bron didn't want to call his office. Things were bad enough already; the others didn't need to know about Neil not coming home. She couldn't, wouldn't, call Maureen again. Maybe Neil was drunk. Maybe he had had a car accident.

It was Peter who told Bron what Mark had told me. Bron wept. "It's better to be prepared," Peter said. "Maybe Neil called someone and learned it would be public soon. Maybe he just needs time."

"I wish I didn't know," Bron wept. "I kept hoping and hoping it would all go away, just disappear! Oh, God, what if Neil's killed himself?"

"He wouldn't do that," Peter said. "I bet you'll find that he merely needed some time to himself."

"Why didn't he send for a limo for Juliana?"

"Because he needed to get away," Peter said.

"Away from me," Bron said. "But if I wasn't here he'd be worse."

Finally Peter looked at his watch and announced that he'd take Conrad, who was in the car, for a walk.

"I'm sorry Peter told you," I said, when he was gone. "Tonight of all times."

Bron lit another cigarette. The air was blue.

"Maybe it's better to know and to be prepared," she said. "Do you think Neil would be better off without me here?"

"It's good you're here. I can't imagine anyone going through something like this alone. You and Neil go back a long way."

"We've been getting closer again," Bron said. "We... uh... shared a bed." She blushed, but looked right at me. "I never thought that would happen. We went through such bad times. You have no idea. Neil made it plain it was all over between us. I felt the same way. I don't think we'll get back together, not really, and it probably meant nothing. But we're like a pair of old slippers."

"Maybe you'll reconcile," I said.

"I don't know if I want to," Bron said, pushing away from the table and going to look out of the kitchen window, as if Neil might suddenly appear. "We've both had other partners. He had someone living here. I was involved with my fellow, Jack. I might have married Jack if he hadn't died. We're different people now. I'm not that innocent young woman who was starry-eyed at getting an engagement ring and he's not the dashing young cop racing around in his cruiser. I thought I was nuts about him." She dropped the curtain. "But I think I was in love with his image. What a dope I was. When the uniform came off, he was like everyone else.

"I like him much better today," she added.

Peter went home at one. I stayed. We sat up until three while Bron talked about her early days with Neil. Tucked in on the couch, I was awake until four, listening for the sound of Neil's car.

In the morning, Bron reported Neil as missing.

It was the worst thing she could have done.

Chapter Twelve

Helena had been murdered. Her body was found in a park near her apartment. She had been shot in the head.

RAPE VICTIM MURDERED. It made the evening news. A woman who alleged an OPP officer had raped her seven years before had been found fatally wounded behind a row of cedar trees in a nearby park.

As Mark had promised, a friend of Helena's, a chubby woman with red hair, told the camera that Helena had been distraught about having to testify in court about her assault. Helena had received threatening phone calls and was considering dropping the action as she feared for her life.

"Pictured is Neil Andersen, the man the victim alleges raped her." A smiling shot of Neil, leaning on his cruiser, his eyes crinkling in that familiar way, flashed across the screen.

"It was a horrendous experience for her, horrendous and devastating," the friend said. "It affected her whole life. She's been suffering from nightmares and has been unable to work. She was unhappy and depressed."

Police were investigating.

And looking for Neil Andersen, who had not been seen since Monday morning, "when he drove a visitor to the airport."

I cancelled next day's class. I was still at Bron's, although I had gone home for a change of clothes and to feed Willy. I hadn't read the assignments and hadn't done any preparatory work. Someone had to stay with Bron until Maureen arrived.

Maureen *was* coming. She had taken a leave of absence from the women's centre and Bruce tersely told Bron on the phone that he thought, "There has to be something to this or why would he disappear at the same time as the victim was killed?" But Maureen was coming to be with her mother.

It got worse. The murder weapon was found. It was Neil's service revolver.

"At least he didn't shoot himself with the gun," Bron said.

And then Neil gave himself up.

He had, Bron told me after she talked to him at the Toronto detention centre, driven around Toronto after Juliana's flight left. He had called Jane, who was still using her maiden name and whose number was in the directory, and they met for lunch. After that, Neil drove aimlessly around Toronto, trying to think. He stopped in Yorkville, where he chatted with strangers in a bar and had a few drinks. The drinks went right to his head and he took a hotel room, where he slept around the clock.

And then he heard on TV that Helena had been shot. It was crazy and not thought out, but Neil set out for the north, just driving, before he came to his senses and gave himself up.

"Someone must have stolen his gun. It was in the trunk of his car, you know, and he didn't have official permission to sign it out! And doctored his drink," Bron kept saying. And: "Maybe he's suffering from amnesia. Do you think he could be suffering from amnesia? He had the gun in the car and he forgot...

"But I know Neil didn't kill that woman! I don't believe it! He says he didn't and I know he's telling the truth."

It didn't look good to me. Neil's actions— running away, drinking too much— were not the actions of the Neil I knew. Could someone have poisoned him? Or was he just filled with enough despair to flee?

Remorse? Guilt?

Was it possible? I wondered as I heated tomato soup for Bron, who was now saying she wanted a drink. She hadn't eaten all day and I'd gone to the store for her cigarettes.

"Maybe he ran into one of those underworld people he used to know," Bron speculated. "Someone he busted. He could have met someone like that. Bumped into them at that bar. He could have. And then they got his gun and shot that woman..."

It was better than the amnesia theory, I thought.

Maureen Andersen-Morton did not like me.

"Thanks for staying with my mother," she told me. "I know you're busy and you'll be wanting to get back to your own concerns."

Her long, shiny hair swung as she briskly put away the groceries she had brought with her. She was a small, trim woman with Neil's eyes and Bron's snubbed nose, dressed simply in expensive cotton trousers and a long black sweater. I could feel her tension as she emptied Bron's despicable ashtrays.

I had expected a basket case.

"You didn't have to cancel your class after all," Bron said as I pulled my jacket on. "Carolyn teaches the writing class I go to," she told her daughter. "Every Thursday night. I wouldn't have gone tonight anyway."

"You have to face things," Maureen said, folding the plastic bags the groceries had come in. "You can't run away."

The media wasted no time. "OPP Officer Arrested After Rape Victim Murdered" screamed a Toronto tabloid. The evening news flashed the same picture of Neil, leaning on his cruiser. "This woman—" there was Helena, much as Neil had described her, cuddling a dog— "claimed she had been raped seven years ago by Constable Neil Andersen when she worked at the OPP detachment in Leicester." They showed the building. "Two days ago, Helena's body was found in this park—" picture of bushes— "with gunshot wounds to the head. The recovered weapon allegedly belongs to Andersen..."

"She was a lovely girl who was coming to terms with her trauma. Charging Andersen was an important step in her recovery," said the same friend as before. "She hesitated because she feared for her life. I still can't believe it, that she's gone..." The woman wept.

Emma called. Couldn't believe it. Ditto for Bella and Frederick from the class. Scottie phoned and said it had to be a frame-up. Amanda said she was so sorry for the whole family.

Marion phoned. But she didn't discuss Neil.

Hugh had had a heart attack.

He had slumped over in the Ritz Cafe where he went every morning to gossip with the town's businessmen. They were talking about Quebec when Hugh fell over, spilling coffee. Luckily, Henry O'Toole, manager of the hardware store and a swim coach, knew CPR, and was soon filling Hugh's lungs with life-giving air. Within minutes, Hugh was in an ambulance on the way to Meredith's small hospital.

It had been a close call. At sixty-seven, Hugh was overweight and the main exercise he got was doing odd jobs around the house. He enjoyed food, liked his wine and port, and although he had given up smoking before, he had been a pack-a-day man for years.

"He didn't complain," Marion said. "He didn't have chest pains."

"Dad wouldn't have said anyway," Peter said.

We left Guelph right away. It was a four-hour drive to Meredith, and that didn't count a stop for food, but we made it in less than three-and-a-half hours. Peter, usually a cautious driver, went over the speed limit and swore angrily when we were held up outside of Orillia because of an over-turned truck.

Peter and Hugh had had their problems over the years. On Hugh's part, there was an unspoken resentment that Peter was not quite the man's man he would have preferred his son to be. Peter wasn't keen on Hugh's good-old-boy British mentality, and growing up as the Police Chief's son— a Limey Police Chief's son— caused teasing and schoolyard fights.

I knew what Peter was thinking: what if Dad dies before we get there? What if he dies, period? I had the same feeling of disbelief when my grandmother died. She was in her late eighties, but her death left a void. She had always been there. And then, she wasn't. You couldn't call the death of a very old woman a tragedy, but to me it had been just that. She did not regain consciousness while I sat by her bed for a week after she suffered a major stroke. The doctor spoke about brain damage. But I wanted her to live, and when she stopped breathing, it seemed unbelievable that I would never see her again.

Even Conrad was quiet on the drive north.

We went straight to the hospital. Peter gripped my hand and his voice shook when he made enquiries at the front desk. Peter had gone to school with Nancy, the receptionist.

"We've got your dad in 203. Wasn't that something? What a shock for you! I couldn't believe it. Your mother's with him now."

"He's all right?"

"They've just moved him out of Intensive Care."

Hugh was groggy, but awake. His face was flushed and there was an intravenous line in his hand. He was hooked up to a monitor. Marion sat by the bed. Marion had gotten younger and younger looking over the years, mainly because of dressing in a more trendy way— polyester and pastel knits replaced by cotton and earth tones— but today her wrinkles showed.

"Bloody business," Hugh mumbled. "What're you doing here?"

"We came to see you. You don't look so bad," Peter said, but he blinked back tears behind his glasses.

Hugh closed his eyes.

"I suppose they're going to keep me in here."

"They want to run some tests," Marion said. "You'll be home in no time at all."

I hadn't expected Marion to be distraught; had, in fact, found it impossible to imagine how she would be if we got there and Hugh had died. Marion wasn't a weeper and a wailer and there was always a calming atmosphere around her. For years she had remained in the background as the Police Chief's wife, knitting, reading millions of books and keeping apart from the small town "nonsense" as she called it; she wasn't a joiner.

She kept reaching for Hugh's hand.

"Allison's arriving later," she told us.

"Wasn't it her weekend with Steven?" I asked. "She didn't call me about the boys, though."

With all the worry about Neil, I'd forgotten about Allison's regular visit to Kingston.

"She didn't mention Kingston to me. Did you bring Conrad?"

Hugh opened his eyes and closed them.

"The pooper's in the car," Peter said.

"Dogs not allowed in the hospital," Hugh mumbled.

Marion and Peter insisted that everything would be fine. Hugh would have to watch his diet, Marion said, back at the house. No more bacon, cut down on the eggs. He had to have his bacon and eggs every morning, no matter what! And the coffee! Two cups before Hugh went to the Ritz and she had no idea how many cups of the obscenely strong brew he swallowed there! He was swimming in caffeine, Hugh was! And as for gravy, a meal without gravy wasn't a meal to Hugh!

"Maybe now he'll listen," Marion said.

"Just don't buy the stuff," Peter said.

"The tourists expect it."

"He'll just have to learn," Peter insisted.

"You know your dad."

"Stubborn."

"He has always been that way."

Back and forth the litany went, as if they had to reassure themselves that Hugh was all right. Alive. Discussing his quirks, they could not be mourning him. It was something deeper, too: affirming the bond that existed in the family, something that I, no matter how close I was to Marion and to Peter, had little part of in a primal, flesh-and-blood way.

They were still talking when Allison and the boys arrived.

"Well, now, Dad's all right." Marion patted Allison's back and said something about a cup of tea.

"Tea! Is that all you can think about?" Allison cried. "How is he? Did you see him?"

"He's his own self," Peter said. "Blustering away."

"But what did the doctor say?" Allison wanted to know.

Matthew was at the fridge, drinking milk out of the carton. He always did this and Marion always snapped at him. Tonight she ignored him. Matthew wiped his mouth with the back of his hand. He was close to Hugh and looked pale as he poked my shoulder.

"They have to run tests, to see what damage has been done," Marion said, plugging in the kettle.

"I got here as fast as I could. The van was in the shop." Allison wiped her face with a crumpled kleenex. "I'm going to the hospital."

Matthew wanted to go, too.

Marion dropped a teacup; it shattered on the floor.

In the end, Marion, Peter, Allison and Matthew went to the hospital. I stayed with Jody and Timmy. And, as Peter reminded me, Conrad hadn't had his evening walk.

I had come to like Meredith over the years. Once it had seemed poky and dusty, just another northern town with one main street of stores, a few streets of brick houses where the affluent (read bank manager, doctor) lived, and an assortment of lanes and roads with potholes where new bungalows mingled with older, frame houses, many of them with strange additions, and all of them with stacked woodpiles in preparation for winter.

Marion and Hugh's cozy house with its large, chintzy rooms, books, plants and good cooking smells seemed like home from the beginning, but it took time to grow familiar with the town. Now, the store clerks recognized me. Peter and I often drank beer at the Meredith Hotel, where he'd run into old schoolmates. I knew the town gossip: who was going to run for mayor, who was said to be having an affair.

Marion and I always— unless she had a houseful of tourists staying— had lunch at the Ritz. But not this Saturday. When I got up at nine, I was surprised to find she had already driven to the hospital in her yellow VW.

"I'll be going later," Allison told me, scrambling eggs for the boys' breakfast. "I thought you could bring the kids over to say hello. Dad's not supposed to have a lot of company, but I know they'll cheer him up. I want to talk to the doctor today."

"What a shock it must have been for you, Allison."

She took the pan off the stove. "I had a feeling something would happen. It was my weekend to go to Kingston, but I called Steven Thursday and told him I couldn't make it. Too much work, I said, which was true."

"ESP," I said.

"I was always close to Dad when I was growing up." She dished out the eggs. Once she would not have talked to me this way. "Things sort of changed when I married Joe. I guess Dad was disappointed. But now we're close again."

"You never stop being close. It just seems that way."

"Yeah, I know what you mean. Where's Peter?"

"Out with Conrad. Matthew, too."

"Figures." She called Jody and Timmy from the den, where they were watching TV. "Peter and Dad, now, that was a different story. I think I should have been the boy. When Peter was fourteen and fifteen he could do nothing right. I used to call him a sissy. What a nerd. It drove Dad wild. But you can tell Dad's heart attack really has Peter worried."

"I know."

"I see it at Mac all the time. Families draw closer when something like this happens. They forget old grievances. Come on, you guys!!! Those kids!"

She flew into the den and snapped the set off.

"I guess Dad being the Chief of Police had something to do with it," she continued as the boys started— grudgingly— "Eat the eggs! There's no Captain Crunch here—" on their breakfast. "And speaking of the police, Peter told me about Neil on the way back from the hospital last night."

"About the woman being shot? You didn't hear on the news? Read the paper?"

"Nope. We have a new policy. No TV on school nights. Steven's influence. And I've been too busy studying to bother with the paper."

"He didn't do it. I know he didn't."

"It seems pretty improbable to me. He's such a nice guy. But they did find his gun, Peter said."

"It's all some terrible mistake," I said, as Peter and Matthew returned with Conrad. And then Allison forgot about Neil.

After the grown-ups left for the hospital, I dialled Bron's number. There was no answer.

Chapter Thirteen

It appeared that Hugh would be all right, but Peter was reluctant to return to Guelph. Allison left Monday morning at six because she had an exam. If Peter went, Marion would be alone.

"Why don't you stay?" I suggested as we walked Conrad Monday morning along Main Street. The mail hadn't been picked up from the post office since Thursday and there was banking to be done. Combining these chores with giving the pooper his morning exercise was a good idea, but it meant we couldn't stop at the Ritz for coffee. "I'll drive down later today. I could even return on the weekend to pick you up. The store's in good hands and I'll fill in when Carrie has a class."

Carrie Decker was a part-time mature student at the University of Guelph. A teenager, Phil, helped on the weekends, but Carrie kept things going if we had to be away.

"Your mother could use the company," I said. "She's got too much on her mind to go home to an empty house after the hospital."

"What about Conrad?"

"He can stay here."

"You sure? You sure you'll be all right?" He jerked Conrad's leash to get him away from a pizza crust on the sidewalk. Conrad strained. "Stop it, you idiot! No!"

"Of course I'll be all right."

"What about that Suzanne woman?"

"I'll just have to take my chances," I said. "I'll call the cops if she causes trouble again."

"I suppose you couldn't cancel the class?" Peter speculated.

"I already cancelled last week. It's not as if—" *someone died.*

Peter knew what I meant.

"You'll feel better with Conrad here," I said. "For company."

"I wish you hadn't taken the class on."

"I know. I'd like to stay in Meredith, too."

"I don't *have* to stay. It's not as if Dad won't be home soon."

"I think you should stay, especially since Allison had to leave."

"She should have stayed."

"She had to write that exam."

"Couldn't you wait until tomorrow to leave? That would still give you time to get ready for the damn class."

"I'll wait until tomorrow."

"And then you'll take Conrad with you," Peter said.

The problem with waiting until the next day was that I had forgotten to put out fresh kibble for Willy. I had filled his bowl to the brim, but would that see him through? The water bowl was full, too, and surely he wouldn't waste away... but what if he did? I was certain the basement door was shut; he couldn't reach the upstairs bathroom and drink out of the toilet bowl...

It was, considering Hugh's heart attack, absurd to worry about a cat—a cat did have nine lives; there were stories about cats who survived inside walls and trunks for days and days, but as I drove home, I had a terrible feeling about Willy. Why hadn't I called Emma from Meredith to ask her to go over to feed Willy? Or Scottie? Both knew we hid a spare key to the front door under the wrought-iron planter on the porch.

I had dreamt about Willy during the night. He was washing his feet and looking at me reproachfully. Then he was in my arms, snuggling in, lifting his little cat face to gaze at me with his yellow eyes. I could feel his fur against my chin and when I awoke suddenly I was sure a cat was walking across the top of the bed. I must have said something because Peter sat up and cried, "What? What? What's happened?"

It was a mystery to me why I kept Willy a secret. Despite Peter's grumbling, he wouldn't have thrown Willy out or sent him off to the Humane Society. Conrad would have gotten used to a cat sooner or later.

But there seemed to be a special link between the orphaned cat and me. Could it be, was it possible, that I didn't want to share Willy with someone else?

I was glad I had Conrad with me when I got home. Someone had thrown a large rock through the side window in the kitchen.

The basement door was open. At least Willy had had his freedom while I was in Meredith.

But Willy was gone.

I called Scottie, who could fix just about anything. A trip to Home Hardware, and presto, the glass was soon replaced.

"I know it was that 'Suzanne woman,' as Peter calls her," I told Scottie. I had made tea, defrosted scones, and fetched the whiskey, which I added liberally to our Earl Grey. "I suppose I should call the police."

I told Scottie the story about the fight on the street.

"Should have called them before the damage was repaired," Scottie said philosophically. "For fingerprints and such."

"There would hardly be fingerprints on the glass. But I have the rock."

We both looked at it. It sat on the counter, a heavy grey stone that looked as if it had come from someone's rock garden.

"Should I call the police?" I asked Scottie.

"I would say so. Yes, I would indeed."

"She will just deny it. What if there are no fingerprints? Then she'll harass me worse than before. Damn the bitch! Last time it was just a patch of hair. Maybe she'll burn the house down next. She should be locked up!" I cried, forgetting for the moment about Scottie's mother.

Scottie poured himself more whiskey and changed the subject. Even Conrad was affected, he said, patting his knee to bring Conrad over.

But Conrad continued pacing and whining, sniffing the floor.

Where a rock had fallen, and where a cat had walked.

I called the Guelph Police, who took almost an hour to arrive. By that time, Scottie was mellow with whiskey and Conrad's antsiness came to a head when he saw the uniforms. I had to shut him up in the bedroom.

I had already, of course, told the police about the flat tire and the phone calls. This time, I informed them about the fight on the street.

Did I want to press assault charges?

No. I just wanted the woman to leave me alone.

"Can't you just sort of— warn her?" I asked, knowing they probably could not do any such thing. There was no evidence linking her to the thrown rock. Of course, they would check for fingerprints, interview the neighbours, and check the yard for footprints, but I doubted if this crime, which hardly qualified as major, would be solved.

But what a shame I hadn't gone to the hospital after the assault, the young police officer told me, closing her notebook. There would have been enough evidence to secure a conviction.

"I felt so silly," I told her. "Fighting in the street."

"Sorry?"

Conrad was barking behind the bedroom door. I shook my head.

"Next time I'll report it," I said loudly.

"Let's hope there won't be a next time," the constable said.

"I'm going to take Conrad around the block," I told Scottie. "Help yourself to the whiskey. You might as well stay for supper. There's some chili in the freezer I can defrost in the microwave."

Conrad pulled and tugged in the direction of the walk under the kitchen window. It took all my strength to drag him away in the opposite direction.

"Willy? Where are you, Willy?"

"Meow, Willy, meow, kittie!"

Conrad went nuts. Why had I taken him along? He gave me an incredulous look and went diving under bushes, barking at trees and lunging at shadows. CAT? Had I said CAT?

At the corner of Lancaster and Beaver, he spied a small black CAT and suddenly the leash was out of my hands as he streaked across the street and sent the cat under a porch. I knew the people slightly: the Simpsons. Conrad had dumped on their lawn more than once. I was reaching for the leash when their front light came on.

"Sorry. I'm afraid Conrad saw your cat... I'm really sorry!"

Cat? They didn't have a cat! They would never have a cat! There were enough cats around in the neighbourhood already! Awful cats who were always digging in the garden. Why couldn't people control their pets? they asked. Shouted, rather, because Conrad kept barking at the space under the porch.

I finally pulled Conrad away. Even if Willy was lurking nearby, having escaped through the broken window, he wouldn't come now.

At home, Scottie was watching the evening news. The level of the whiskey bottle was down. I went into the bedroom and called the Humane Society to see if "a neutered orange-and-white male cat" was at the shelter.

No such creature was there.

I wanted Scottie to spend the night. He seemed okay after two large bowls of chili, rolls, three cups of tea and a handful of Oreo cookies, but I worried about the whiskey he'd had.

"Och no, I'm fine. Can't leave the puppy home alone now, can I?"

"How about if I drive out and pick up Lady, then? You could both stay."

"Well, now, I don't know..."

"I really wouldn't mind. I'll drive to your place, fetch Lady, and we'll have a nightcap later."

It didn't take much to persuade Scottie. He was lonely since his mother had gone "away." Peter and I used to speculate about Scottie and women. After we learned he was gay, we wondered if Scottie would ever find a companion, but he seemed to have gotten used to his solitary ways.

I was tempted to ask him if I could use his truck, but the question would embarrass him. He'd let me have it— reluctantly. He was fussy about his ancient vehicle, forever having it repaired. He had even done bodywork on it himself before taking it to the paint shop.

I would just have to take my chances that that "damn Suzanne" wasn't around to recognize my car, which she would follow to Scottie's country road.

Scottie hadn't left any lights burning ("A penny saved," I remembered Mabel saying) and I could hear Lady barking within the dark house as soon as I got out of the car. At least I didn't have to worry about Lady, who knew me well and generally peed— now that she was old— with delight as soon as she saw me.

She was all over me at once.

"There, there, Lady! You're coming home with me, girl!"

She looked at me, trying to understand, trotted obediently to the door, and sat down to wait for me while I looked around the kitchen. Clean dishes stood in the drainer and were covered neatly with a striped tea towel. Scottie kept the place clean. The only un-Mabel note was the bottle of Scotch on the sideboard. In Mabel's day it was kept in the cupboard.

"Okay, girl, let's go see Scottie."

Lady's tail thumped. She smiled at me. The phone rang.

It was Bron.

"Carolyn? What're you doing there?"

"I didn't know you knew Scottie!"

"I don't. But Neil talked about him, how you bought Conrad there. I think you mentioned Scottie, too. I thought this Scottie would know where you were."

"Peter's father had a heart attack. We had to go to Meredith." After listening to her expressions of surprise and sympathy, I explained what I was doing at Scottie's. "Is Maureen still with you?"

"No, she went back. We... ah... sort of had an argument. It's a long story."

Lady whined plaintively at the door.

"And a big mess," Bron went on. "A helluva mess..."

"It must be difficult for Maureen, too. I mean, with Bruce."

"He's part of the problem. Listen, I know it's a lot to ask but... Can you drive me to Toronto tomorrow?"

"What?"

"I'm going to that bar where Neil was! Oh, Carolyn, I wouldn't ask you, but I'm desperate. If you're busy I'll take the train, but I thought..."

Tomorrow was Wednesday. The class was Thursday. I could stay up tonight, I decided, and prepare for the class. I didn't have a lot to read, and, I decided right then to talk about submissions on Thursday. That wouldn't take much preparation, only getting together books on writers' markets and various magazines.

"I'll have to check on the store first, but I guess we could leave after that," I told Bron.

Lady barked gently.

"I'll call you at eleven after I've called Carrie at the store. It should be all right."

"I can't thank you enough, Carolyn. Neil asked about you, by the way. He was so relieved that you believe in him. Oh, I'm so glad I found you!"

"Why didn't you leave a message on the machine?"

"It wasn't on! The phone rang and rang!"

"Are you sure? Maybe you had the wrong number. There were several messages on the machine." Jake had called about an anthology, and there was a reminder from the vet that Conrad was due for his annual shots. And several people had hung up without leaving messages.

"No, I kept calling and calling. I was getting worried," Bron said.

After Scottie and I took the dogs for a walk, we finished what was left of the whiskey.

Scottie, with Lady draped across his lap, was mellow. He even talked about his mother.

"Life is a mystery. Who knows the ABCs or the why's and wherefore's, eh, Carolyn? Mother's away and I'm off to Scotland on me own. Never thought things would turn out this way. Your friend's in jail and Peter's dad has almost met the man with the sickle. Never do we know, never never in God's creation do we know what tomorrow will bring." He stroked Lady's ears and looked at Conrad, who was sleeping peacefully in the old armchair we had bought at a yard sale.

"It's the beasties who are fortunate. They do not think of tomorrow. Bit of affection, their bowls of food, and they are happy and content. Why am I going to the old country? Can you tell me, lass? We were going together, Mother and I, and now I am going alone. I should be satisfied with my own place and my own dog by the fire. Instead..."

He shook his head.

"Does your mother know you're going to Scotland?"

"She is worried the plane will crash, and then who will visit her."

"I'll visit her, Scottie," I told him. "And Lady can stay here while you're away. Of course you must go."

"And will they believe me when I say Mother's not well?"

"Why shouldn't they believe that? Your mother's not a young woman."

"But not an old one. Her mother lived to ninety-nine. Mother has many years left yet."

"How's she coping?" I had never dared to ask this before.

"She is teaching knitting. She is happier these days. Her health has improved. Her worry is that her sister will find out, but I mail the letters from Guelph. You would do the same?"

"Of course I would!"

Scottie poured out the last of the whiskey.

"Let us hope our Neil does not face Mother's predicament," he said.

Chapter Fourteen

Before Scottie left in the morning, he found the cat dishes and the bag of kibble in the basement. Or, more specifically, he caught Conrad eating the kibble. I had finally located the American writers' market guide in a box in the basement and had, in my whiskey-fogged mind, forgotten to close the door.

This was all right while Conrad was asleep, but Scottie was up early to make his tea and heard Conrad crunching and chomping away downstairs. Conrad was demolishing the empty bag, with a disapproving Lady looking on, by the time Scottie came downstairs.

"So that is what all that whining was about last night," Scottie said, after I told him about Willy. "I had forgotten about the cat. Was it not at Peter's store?"

"It was, then it wasn't. I found him at Mrs. Maloff's house and brought him here. Now he's gone."

"Likely jumped through the broken window," Scottie said. "Well, he may be back and he may not. I would not worry. If he is meant to come back, he will come back. Not like dogs, cats."

"Don't tell Peter."

"A secret, is it?"

"Not a secret. I just didn't feel like telling him yet."

"Maybe you will not have to tell him. Ever."

"I hope you're wrong. I got so used to that little guy. I wish Conrad hadn't gotten into the food, though. How can I go to Toronto with Bron with that load in his belly?"

"I'll check on the fellow at noon."

"I don't want Conrad in the back yard. That Suzanne could come along, and you never know."

"I could leave Lady as well. I was planning on taking her on the job today, but she might as well keep your Conrad company."

"You take Lady to work?"

"Now and again. She's a favourite, is Lady. But don't you worry about a thing. I'll look after the pups. You go to that Toronto and do your best for our Neil."

Yes, I was going to Toronto. Carrie said she didn't need help at the store.

Chapter Fifteen

Bron wanted to go to the Quartet, the hotel where Neil had stayed, and then we were meeting Neil's ex-girlfriend, Jane, whose old business card Bron found among a bunch of letters in Neil's top dresser drawer. It wasn't hard to track Jane down— she still worked for the same firm.

The Quartet Hotel was in the old Yorkville area of Toronto, which had been a hippie haunt in the late sixties and early seventies. Today, Yorkville is chic with boutiques, art galleries and cafes.

The Quartet Hotel looked newish, a middle-of-the-road place, not as convenient as the larger inns on Harbourfront with their easy access to the downtown and the airport, and not as old-world posh as the Royal York.

It was just enough out of the way that I could imagine Neil, driving around the city and coming upon the eight-storey structure, saying, "To Hell With It," and deciding to stop for a drink. There was no underground parking. He would have left his car in the lot just down the street, where it would have been easy for someone to get to it. *To steal his gun*, Bron said, brightening as I locked the Volvo.

The lobby was red and gold, with crystal chandeliers overhead and smart pages in red uniforms. The effect was meant to be luxurious, rich, but there was something vulgar about it, as if the decorator had tried to show opulence, but had no idea how to do it.

A woman in a mink coat, perfumed and coiffed, sailed past us and ignored the doorman who held the door for her. A Japanese businessman in an immaculate navy suit was signing in at the concierge's desk.

A discreet sign, in gold lettering, led the way to the Mozart Lounge. The Oak Dining Hall was on the opposite side of the lobby, with windows facing the street.

"I guess the place to start with is the Mozart Lounge," I said.

We stepped into a darkish room with wooden beams and leather chairs grouped around round tables. Pictures of the composer and European village scenes covered the walls. A baby grand stood in the corner.

There was no one at the bar where the bartender stood polishing glasses, but... Robert Browning, a Hendricks author I had introduced to the firm, was drinking dark ale at one of the tables.

His round, chubby face creased into that boyish grin of his when he saw me. The red turtleneck he wore made him look like a Christmas elf. He lifted his stein and motioned us over.

I had met Robert ("the other Robert Browning") at McMaster Hospital in Hamilton. He was a minister visiting a dying parishioner, and, it turned out, a great fan of mine and a secret writer of mystery novels. I read his manuscripts, which were hilarious tales about a pastor, and recommended them to Jake, who went on to publish several of Robert's novels. The books had done well, and Jake told me in the summer that Robert was taking a year off from the church.

"Well, well, well! Surprises never cease! Sit down, sit down!"

After introductions, Robert ordered another ale for himself ("Nothing like sinning in the morning!") and coffee for Bron and me.

"I never expected to see you here," I told Robert.

"Research, research. For the ambience and the detail. I've been coming here for months. Spend a night or two to soak up the atmosphere. I'm thinking of a new series set in a hotel."

"Goodbye to your pastor?"

"Goodbye to my pastor, but hello to my bell hop. He's a Renaissance man who has run out of options, you see. Or a woman hotel manager. I'm not sure yet. Did you get the invitation to my launch in November?"

"Not yet, but I saw the new mystery listed in the catalogue. You're doing a book a year, it seems. I guess I have writers' block myself."

We spent some time doing the obligatory literary talk. Bron smoked a cigarette. I told Robert about Bron attending my class, but she didn't join in the conversation, and after the bartender refilled our coffee cups, she took a picture of Neil out of her purse and showed it to Robert.

Robert shook his head. It wasn't the picture in the news, but a shot of Neil casually dressed in jeans and an open-necked shirt, taken in his back yard.

"That's my ex-husband and he's been charged with murder," Bron said. "He's with the OPP. It was in the news. A girl accused Neil of rape and then she was killed."

Robert studied the photo. He didn't seem fazed by Bron's direct words.

"I'm sorry. There's so much violence in the media. It's hard to remember."

"One murder more or less, what's the difference?" Bron sounded bitter.

"We know Neil's innocent," I told Robert. "He's been a good friend for a long time. You may have met him at the hospital in Hamilton that time."

"My ex-husband *is* innocent," Bron said.

"I am sorry. I didn't mean to imply that I'm indifferent," Robert told Bron. It was easy to see the clergyman in him. "But I've been pretty much holed up with my writing, you see. I've even stopped watching television; it's too distracting. I do wish I could help you. And yes, I may have met him at McMaster Hospital."

"Neil stayed here when the woman was murdered. He drank in this very room," I told Robert and went on to relate the story.

"And if his car was parked down the street, in an open lot," Bron said, "it would have been easy for someone to break into his car and take his gun."

"Or he could have parked underground," Robert said. "There is hotel parking, but the entrance is from the side street. You would not see it from the front, or know about it unless you stayed here. Someone could break into the car in the underground parking, I suppose."

"Only if they knew the car was there." Bron lit a fresh cigarette.

"There is no security in the garage," Robert said. He squinted against the smoke. Bron stubbed the cigarette out. "People come and go. The Quartet is not what it seems. Oh, no. They get the international businessmen and they host conferences, but there is another kind of trade here as well."

"You mean— "

"Ladies of the night, courtesans." Robert nodded his head vigorously and grinned. "High-class ones."

"Escort services? I imagine the escort services deal with most hotels," I said.

"Perhaps so. I only know about the Quartet. I see the same women here. You wouldn't know by looking at them. I was flabbergasted! Glamorous women, not tarty one bit. I wouldn't want to ask what they charge. A pretty penny, I imagine."

"And they look like women you could take home to Mother," I said.

"Not to my mother! Oh, dear, no. No, no. Mother would have a stroke!"

"But Neil could have picked a woman up!" Bron said. "Don't you see?" she asked me. "He knew hookers when he worked undercover. She could have remembered him. Maybe he busted her. But he doesn't remember her. So they have a few drinks and he tells her his troubles and she goes and shoots the woman."

"I don't think the pathetic girls standing on street corners have anything to do with these— courtesans." I chose Robert's word.

"She could have come up in the world. Met a powerful man, say. Someone with criminal connections. The Mafia type. So she gets off drugs or whatever or maybe she uses blackmail to get somewhere and learns how to dress, what fork to use. She's really glamorous now and Neil wouldn't recognize her even if he did remember her."

Bron was off.

"Neil was on the prostitution beat when he was undercover. Get them off the streets, you know? Arrest the johns, too. But mainly it was drugs. These girls worked the streets so they could pay for their habits. Worked for pimps, too, they did. It was a terrible world, girls of fourteen and fifteen with track marks up their arms, girls sent out by pimps who would beat them if they didn't bring in enough. Neil felt so sorry for them. The courts would send them to group homes, but within weeks they'd be on the streets again.

"You'd think only bums would be interested in these wraiths but Neil said Cadillacs would stop, rich businessmen who wanted a blow job for ten dollars. The police even set up undercover woman cops to act as hookers. Not that it did much good. There were always more girls. And the men, the johns! Imagine being a stockbroker and having to go to court for offering money for sex!"

Robert took out a notebook. Details, he said; ideas. These were not things he was familiar with in his life as a clergyman in middle-class and rural churches. Oh, he had known runaways and kids who drank, but his experience with the women Bron was talking about was zilch. Zilch.

Bron cut him off. Neil had been threatened by several businessmen. Someone tried to sue. He hadn't returned to Toronto for years in case someone recognized him.

Didn't we see? Neil had met someone who knew him from before! She spiked his drink, got him to his room and broke into his car. Or took the car, even! While Neil slept, the woman killed Helena, having found out about her from Neil.

But how would she know where to find Helena? Robert asked.

"Connections," Bron said. "Maybe even connections within the police force. A policeman was even arrested when Neil was undercover!

The Toronto police didn't know he was OPP, you see. Neil didn't know where Helena lived, but the police would have known!"

"How would she have recognized this Helena?" Robert wanted to know.

"If she found out where she lived, she would have followed her."

It was a shaky premise, but possible, I admitted to myself as Bron walked over to the bar, where she handed the bartender Neil's picture.

"Dave won't tell her anything," Robert said. "He might give information to the police, but I rather doubt that, too. Look."

Dave's face was impassive as he looked at Neil's picture.

"Now is when in novels and detective shows you're supposed to slip the guy a hundred bucks," I said.

"So what do you think? Did the guy do it?"

"All my instincts say he didn't. He's a nice guy. A kind and decent person. But the evidence seems damning. Poor Bron. She's a recovered alcoholic, by the way. I hope she won't start drinking again. If she gets through this, she'll get through anything."

"But they are divorced," Robert mused.

"They're living under one roof. As housemates." I thought of what Bron had told me about her night with Neil. Still, they hadn't really reconciled. But who knew what might happen in the future?

"People do strange things," Robert said. He put the notebook away. "I wouldn't write things down if there were more people around, by the way. Too many people here with people they should not be with. I do, however, write in my room. Writing in a hotel room is deliciously decadent! Ah, here's our friend!"

He stood up when Bron returned to our table.

"He didn't recognize Neil. He wanted me to leave the picture, says he'll show it around. I'll have to get colour photocopies made."

"There's a place down the street," Robert said. "Leave copies with me if you like. I'll ask around. They know me here. And if there's anything else I can do..."

"Neil's father was a minister," Bron said. "He's dead now, but his mother's still alive."

"Oh, dear. It would be difficult for her. Would you like me to visit your husband? I'd be only too glad to do so."

"It's kind of you, but Neil doesn't want visitors for the time being."

"I can understand that."

"How did you discover this place?" I asked Robert.

"Providence. I had a book-signing in the city, and some other business, and looked in the telephone directory at the library. My goodness, I only wanted a quiet, reasonably priced hotel, and certainly never imagined landing in this gold mine, this veritable spring of information and atmosphere. And— by the way, if you don't mind, please don't mention— in case you talk to someone— that I am a clergyman. It's not that I'm ashamed, but people do tend to watch what they say around me if they know."

"Better a raunchy novelist," I said.

"It wasn't a wasted trip," Bron said as we drove north to meet Jane. "Maybe your friend will find someone who admits seeing Neil. I thought that bartender seemed shifty. He wouldn't meet my eyes. And that girl in the restaurant didn't even look at the picture."

"Somehow Robert inspires trust," I said. "Maybe because he's so innocuous and nerdy."

"He is nothing like Neil's father. Neil's dad had a silver moustache and wore tweed. You'd think people wouldn't take Robert seriously with that grin of his."

"People seem to like him. Maybe it's better if the minister doesn't look like Jehovah Himself."

"That's what Neil used to call his father!" Bron cried. "Jehovah Himself!"

"You sound happier today, Bron. More in control."

"I am more in control. I told Maureen to get lost. She wanted me to move to her place. She's taken a leave of absence from work and we'd be at each other's throats. Plus, asshole Bruce is there." She shook her head. "I don't even mind meeting Jane."

"Neil never talked about Jane. I just know they lived together," I said.

"She claimed they'd grown apart, that she wasn't ready for a commitment, but then she turns around and marries a lawyer within six months. If you ask me, she realized Neil wasn't going to set the world on fire. And he was fifteen years older than her. Maureen never liked Jane, said she had charts on the fridge about who would dust and take out the trash.

"Actually, I've always wondered what she was like."

I was curious about Jane, too.

Jane was sleek. Her expensive, sculpted blonde bob was bent over a Caesar salad when we walked into the Market Bistro with its rustic decor. Market scenes from all over the world hung on a brick wall and bushel baskets of potatoes and apples stood about. A treadle sewing machine held an old-fashioned cash register.

Jane extended a slim, tapered hand with manicured, colourless fingernails. Her briefcase sat on the floor and her cellular phone was on the table.

Navy suit, white silk shirt. A clean, cool face and pale gold eyes. The word "lemony" came to mind, and I couldn't imagine her with Neil. Not in the kitchen. Not in the rec room where Neil ate potato chips and watched the Toronto Maple Leafs on television. And not in the bedroom.

Bron and I sat down on the black wrought-iron chairs and Bron's nose began to bleed. Where was kleenex? She fumbled through her purse, spilling keys, a paperback Agatha Christie, Rolaids, a leaky Bic pen, a dirty comb, and lipstick.

"Oh, for heaven's sake!" She cupped her nose while I searched unsuccessfully through my purse.

"Here. I always carry tissue." Jane extracted a baggie containing neatly folded kleenex from her briefcase.

Bron, wobbly in her polyester pants, fled to the washroom.

"She should put her head back," Jane said. She shut her case.

"Bron has allergies. I hope they're not acting up," I said.

"Surely not. Perhaps she has high blood pressure."

"It wouldn't surprise me these days."

We studied each other.

"I don't know what she expects of me," Jane said, as the waiter came over with menus. "I've already talked to the police. There wasn't much I could tell them, either. The woman must have had delusions about Neil."

"You told the police that?"

"Yes, I did. I also said I saw Neil for about forty-five minutes that day. He was naturally upset. I was surprised to hear from him. They asked if he was ever violent with me. I told them he wasn't."

She ate a piece of lettuce.

"I think Bron merely wants to find out about the day the woman was murdered," I said.

"Neil said his ex had moved back in with him."

"It's only temporary. Until she gets on her feet."

"She used to phone when she was drinking."

"She's not drinking any more. I should go and see if she's all right."

"Neil wanted me to tell her to stop calling. But it was his problem."

She was lying, I thought, as I got up to find Bron. Jane would have snatched the phone away from Neil and yelled at Bron to get lost. Bron, being drunk, wouldn't remember.

In the flowery Ladies, Bron was splashing cold water on her face. She looked awful, white and pasty, especially with a wad of toilet paper stuck up her left nostril. There were water stains on her sweatshirt and her hair was wet.

"You okay?"

"Damn it all to hell! I meet Cinderella and my nose starts bleeding!" She sniffed, yanked the paper out, and peered desolately at her reflection in the mirror.

"She's not so great. I can't see what Neil saw in her."

"Sex," Bron said, sniffing again. "I think the bleeding's stopped at least. What a humiliation!"

"I don't know about the sex," I said. "She seems like a cold fish to me."

"Athletic sex," Bron said. "Did you know they went to Bermuda together? Neil got food poisoning and she was angry at him for spoiling their holiday!"

Jane was glancing at her watch when we returned to the table. "Everything's okay," I said. Bron mumbled something about the cold air. Jane nodded, remarked that she had once had a nose bleed skiing. Having witnessed Bron's disgrace, she seemed friendlier. "But you should have your blood pressure checked," she told Bron.

"Jane was telling me, while you were in the Ladies, that she talked to the police," I informed Bron.

"There wasn't much to tell, I'm afraid." Jane opened her case and extracted her date book. "I always keep notes. Here, see for yourself." She passed the book to Bron. "One-thirty, Neil. He phoned around eleven. I didn't have much time. As you can see, there's a meeting pencilled in at two-fifteen."

"You must have been surprised to hear from him," Bron said, studying the journal.

"I haven't seen him since my wedding."

"He came to your wedding? You invited Neil?"

"Sure. No hard feelings. Why not? He gave us a toaster."

"Not a very imaginative gift," Bron said.

"He wasn't the only one who gave us a toaster. I really don't know what I can tell you. I think Neil merely wanted to have someone to talk to."

"He had just put his neighbour's sister on a plane," I said.

"Yes, the awful Mrs. Maloff's sister. Mrs. Maloff would never talk to me. She disapproved of living in sin."

"Mrs. Maloff was killed by her grandson," I said.

"You shouldn't speak ill of the dead," Jane said airily, "but I still don't have anything good to say about her. I waved at her at first and she'd turn her back. Her daughter-in-law used our phone once to call a friend to pick her up when her car broke down. She wouldn't go back into that house and I can't say I blame her. Mrs. Maloff slapped her face, she said."

"So Neil talked about Mrs. Maloff," Bron said.

"Just in passing. He said he'd been to the airport. He was more concerned with that woman from Leicester making those ridiculous accusations. We've had trouble like that in our office, too. Not that there hasn't been harassment, but the guys are pretty careful these days. They watch what they say."

"We're talking rape here," Bron said. "She accused him of raping her."

"I don't believe it," Jane said. "Never in a million years. The woman had her own agenda— wanted to get back at Neil for some imagined slight. Neil and I were living together during that time. He'd come home on the weekend and he'd leave early Monday morning. It was a drag, a real drag. Neil was exhausted, just sort of hung out Saturday. We'd do a movie Saturday night. Sundays we'd try to catch up on yard work or whatever he was too tired to do Saturday, and then it was time for him to return to Leicester."

"It's a long drive and he'd have been driving all week in Leicester, too," Bron said. "He always needed time to unwind. Just laze around, that's Neil."

"Really? We always made a point of doing something special each weekend," Jane said, contradicting herself.

"Of course it's different with children. Maureen—"

It was time to interrupt the one-upmanship. "Did Neil mention Helena to you when you were living together?" I asked Jane.

"Not a word. When he talked about Leicester it was to complain about being away from home during the week. I never heard about her until Neil told me about her accusations."

"Did Neil say where he was going after he saw you?"

"No, but he wanted me to cancel my appointment. He asked me to go to a bar with him, have a few drinks. But I couldn't cancel. And a smokey bar isn't my idea of a place to spend an afternoon."

"You met here?"

"It's close to the office. And as I said, I didn't have much time."

"Did Neil have a drink here?"

"He had a beer. And a sandwich. I suggested he drive home."

"After Neil left here, he went to the Quartet and it looks like he had one too many," I said.

"Oh, the Quartet. We've had clients from Asia staying there. They like the Hilton better."

"And then Neil took a room," I continued. "He has no memory of anything else."

"He was very, very angry at the woman," Jane said.

"Did you tell the police that?" Bron asked.

"No. I said he was upset, that he needed to talk. But he was angry. He seemed to think that someone had put the woman— Helena— up to it. Someone could have convinced her it happened. Neil said she was a real dog."

"Neil called her a real dog?" I asked.

"I can't remember his exact words. He said she wasn't attractive, kind of ugly, and that she must be a psychological mess. He kept saying he could always run away to Mexico. He said he was going to quit the force, but I've heard that one before."

"Just talk," Bron said.

"No, he meant it. He was going to start a consulting company, focus on security, that kind of thing."

"Did Neil talk about anyone from long ago, when he was working undercover in Toronto?" I asked. "Did he see anyone at the airport, for instance?"

"No, he didn't mention that." Jane turned to Bron. "Neil's company would have flown. With my managerial advice and Neil's inside knowledge of the police, we could have done it. I wouldn't be surprised if he did quit the force if he gets off."

"He will get off because he didn't kill that girl," Bron said.

"I know," Jane said.

"Even though he was, as you put it, 'very, very angry.'"

"Neil didn't know where she lived. He said he wished he could just talk to her, but she was in hiding. His lawyer wouldn't let him talk to her, anyway."

"Did he want you to find her?"

Jane coloured. "I offered to look through our computer files. She might have bought an RRSP or made an investment. After I heard the news, I looked. But there was nothing."

"I bet you didn't tell the police that," Bron said.

"Forget I told you."

"I don't suppose Neil would have called you from the Quartet?" Bron asked.

"I was in a meeting for the rest of the afternoon."

"He didn't leave a message?"

"If he did, I didn't get it. Why are you asking?"

"After he left you, and before he went to that hotel, Neil drove around to where we used to live," Bron informed Jane. "I just thought he might have been more upset, that's all. Visiting happier days, you know? And wanting to cry on your shoulder about that, too."

"I had to get that in," Bron said, as we drove away. "She's still carrying a torch for Neil."

"That's a quaint expression."

"Well, she is. If you ask me, the only reason she agreed to see us is because she wanted to look me over."

"She's history, Bron."

"I know she's history and I don't care. I'm history, too. If only she didn't make me feel so old and ugly. Like a dog. And then I had to get that stupid nosebleed."

"So what? Forget it."

"She didn't tell us anything," Bron said. "Maybe I just wanted to get a look at her, too."

A little farther north, on the way to Willowdale, we came to Bron's old neighbourhood of small bungalows and storey-and-a-halfs. The trees had grown, Bron said, and the small, white clapboard house where she had lived with Neil and Maureen had the upstairs extended with dormers. "It was all new, mostly young couples like us," Bron said. "The women got together every morning in someone's kitchen for coffee. None of us worked. We were always back and forth, borrowing sugar, watching the soaps, giving one another perms..."

I parked, but Bron didn't get out of the car.

"I was happy then, but I didn't know it," Bron said.

Chapter Sixteen

"The two big rules for making submissions are: double-space on one side of the paper and use paper clips instead of staples."

Heads bent as the students wrote down this vital information. Never mind simile and metaphor, or "show, don't tell." Sending work out and having it published was what they really cared about. Few were ready to publish— except for Amanda. She had phoned, all stuffed up with a terrible head cold, to say she wouldn't be there.

But they were avidly taking notes about mastheads, query letters, and sample chapters.

"How do you know they won't steal your work?" Brad asked. Tonight he wore what looked like a new khaki shirt, pristine and starched.

"I've never heard of that happening," I told him. "There are so many submissions, for one thing, and I can't see an editor saying, 'Aha! Here's a masterpiece and I'll make a million with it.'"

"But they could take your idea," Brad persisted.

"Ideas can't be copyrighted. If you're really worried, you can send yourself a copy of your work by registered mail."

How many times had I given this information in workshops? Everyone worried a greedy editor would steal their work.

"They say once you publish it's easier," Bella said, fingering her heavy gold chain. There was a mermaid pendant on the end of it.

"The problem is getting published," Frederick sighed. "If you have to be published to get published, how do you start?"

"I think good work always stands out," I said. "Of course, there are exceptions. A writer in the States, John Kennedy Toole, wrote a wonderful novel, *A Confederacy of Dunces*, he couldn't get published. He committed suicide. After his death, his mother took the manuscript to Walker Percy, a writer who was teaching at a university, I think in Louisiana, and Percy found a publisher. The book won the Pulitzer Prize."

"So it helps to know someone," Frances said. "It's not the quality of the work at all!" Her lips set. She looked around in indignation.

"Knowing a writer with an in doesn't automatically mean the book will be published. It depends on the work, if the editor thinks it's marketable. All kinds of things."

Questions continued.

What about agents?

How did you get an agent?

Should you pay an agent?

Do you have any say about the cover?

Can you submit to more than one place at a time?

What about stamps for return postage if you send to the States?

Why not just send a diskette? Or e-mail a story?

How about putting your story on the Internet?

What if you never heard from a magazine again?

What if you sent a story to several magazines and they all wanted to publish it?

Had I had a lot of rejection slips in my life?

"These are all practical and valid concerns," I said. "But I've always found that the writing is one thing, quite divorced from the business side of it. I try not to think about publishing when I write. That's for later. When I first started sending stories out, I did try to tailor them to what the magazines were publishing and none of them sold. Not one. It was a waste of time. An editor from a New York woman's magazine did notice my stories. She liked the writing, but my women characters were always either too young or too old, or too poor. Too something. Or they had inappropriate fantasy lives. The readers of this magazine didn't have fantasy lives, the editor wrote. But that was a long time ago."

"So you turned to cookbooks."

"Quite by accident. I was writing restaurant columns for a small weekly that folded and I began noticing food, how it was prepared, the history of recipes. I added small stories about the women who did the cooking and Hendricks, who is still my publisher, took the first cookbook."

"Out of the slush pile?"

"Sometimes miracles do happen," I said.

I didn't want to go the Berlin Circle. Amanda wouldn't be there and I was tired. I had spent the day at The Bookworm, filling in for Carrie, who had a seminar. And Peter was going to phone later— he had been out when I called earlier. Plus, I had Conrad in the car.

But Bron wanted to go to the Walper.

"Don't worry, I won't get into my cups. Let's just drop in so I can see the place. We don't have to stay long."

What she wished to talk about was, of course, Jane, and as we settled in with our coffee, she told me that Neil had had to take out a second mortgage to buy Jane's share of the house; that Jane had taken tapes Maureen had given Neil for Christmas; that Neil had done most of the cooking.

And so on and so forth. Bron hadn't meant to tell Neil about our meeting with Jane, but it had slipped out when she talked to him. "He did agree she was a cold fish. Do you know how they met? At a bar. It was all hugs and kisses at the beginning, I bet, but he soon learned. She wanted to meet his mother, but Neil wouldn't take her. And I still don't know what she did with our family pictures..."

It was eleven before we left the Walper, and by the time I dropped Bron off at the other end of Guelph, it was almost midnight before I reached home. The phone was ringing. I caught it just before the answering machine cut in.

"My God, where have you been?" Peter wanted to know.

"Bron wanted to go to the Walper after class. I guess she wanted to talk about Jane."

"Jane?"

"Neil's old girlfriend. I drove Bron to Toronto yesterday to meet with her. And guess who we ran into at the hotel where Neil stayed? Robert Browning!"

"What're you doing— playing private eye?"

"Bron really needed to go. And Carrie didn't have a class, so she stayed in the store all day. She'll be in tomorrow, too. As always. But I had to fill in today."

"Hmm. So what's Jane like?"

"Cold and efficient."

"I guess Neil didn't think so at one time. Did you catch the news tonight?"

"Nope. Class, remember?"

"Oh, yeah. They're having a memorial service for that woman tomorrow. Helena."

"Where?"

"At some women's centre. I didn't catch the name. Bron better not think of attending."

"She wouldn't dream of it. Anyway, she won't know about it unless Maureen calls her, and they're not on the best of terms, to put it mildly. But never mind this. How's your father?"

They'd gotten Hugh out of bed that afternoon, Peter told me. He'd be in the hospital another week, but Peter wanted to stay another weekend. Was that okay? Did I mind? I could drive up a week from this weekend to get him.

I didn't mind.

"How's Conrad?"

"He's fine. I took him with me to the class tonight."

"You took him to school?"

"Not in the classroom. He waited in the car." I hadn't told Peter about the stone through our window. Why add to his worries? "He was fine. The same old fool. How's your mother?"

"Better, now that Dad's okay. I think they should close up the bed and breakfast, but she won't hear of it. I told her they should move to Guelph, now that Allison's in Hamilton with the kids, but she says Dad would miss Meredith and all his cronies."

"She's right. Your mother would miss Meredith, too. And she'd miss running the inn."

We discussed this for a while.

"How's Neil?" Peter asked.

"I guess he's hanging in there. Bron talked to him today."

"It'll probably be a zoo at the memorial service," Peter said. "I hope you're not thinking of going."

"Definitely not," I said.

"I hope they have Neil in isolation," Peter said. "He's a dead duck if he's out in the general prison population. There's even talk about him in Meredith."

As soon as I hung up, the phone rang. It was Jane. She'd gotten my number from directory assistance, she said.

Had I seen the news?

"No, I was on my way to Kitchener where I teach a class."

Jane was not interested in my affairs. She began a long monologue about her life with Neil, how wonderful it had been in the beginning, what a decent guy he was, and how she felt they were still friends.

"So what I'm trying to say is that I have real respect for the man. It didn't work out between us, but I understand Neil. I know him inside out, better than his ex. She wasn't what I expected at all. That really was a marriage that went nowhere."

"They were very young when they got married."

"Neil said she was pregnant. It must have been a marriage made in hell. But as I was saying, I understand Neil and—"

I thought of that little house in Toronto. Neil and Bron hadn't always been unhappy. But I wasn't going to argue with Jane.

"—and I thought of going to the memorial service tomorrow. And by the way, after work, I swung around Neil's old place in Toronto. The woman who answered the door recalled Neil's car in front of her house. And someone was around asking about Neil years ago. Isn't that something? She said the woman had frizzy blonde hair. Big hair, she said. She wanted to know where Neil had moved."

"How long ago was this?"

"She wasn't sure. Three years, maybe less. The toughie said she was a friend of Neil's. The present resident of Neil's house had no idea who Neil was and I didn't enlighten her. She didn't make the connection. I told her I was a friend of Neil's from years ago and she said someone else had been looking for him, too."

"The toughie could have been someone Neil knew as a policeman."

"That's exactly my point. And that's why I'm going to the memorial service tomorrow."

"There'll be a lot of women there."

"It's a place to start," Jane said. She sounded business-like and brisk, as if she was ticking off an item on an agenda. "Why don't you come as well?"

I didn't have to think twice.

"Don't bring Bron," Jane said.

Chapter Seventeen

The memorial service for Helena Quintham was held at the Women's House, north of Lawrence Avenue, an area of upscale and trendy antique stores and restaurants, and streets of big old houses. I didn't know this part of Toronto very well, and by the time I found a parking spot on a side street, I only had five minutes before the service.

There was only one television van on the street. The lone cameraman was filming about thirty women carrying signs protesting police power and abuse.

Jane, in a navy suit showing beneath a large trench coat, was waiting in the lobby of a stone building that had obviously once been a church. She seemed more friendly today (because Bron wasn't along?) and ruefully commiserated with me about getting lost.

The vestibule was covered with posters announcing meetings and sessions, but one wall was devoted to a large painting of a sad woman crouched in a chair. Behind her was another woman, naked and strong, with her arms held out.

Were there not police here? I wondered, settling into a metal chair at the back of the large room. The pews had been removed, but the altar, painted yellow and draped with a blue tapestry, remained.

There were women of all ages and— types. Young women with various piercings and violet hair sat beside older ones in comfortable coats. There were a few men and children, too. Beside me, a woman in a cape cradled an infant in a red quilted jumpsuit. The woman who had been on television, talking about Helena, sat near the front.

A pine table near the altar displayed photos of Helena. It was hard to make them out, but a larger one showed a chubby young girl smiling up from a canoe. I recognized the glasses Neil had mentioned. Her face was round, unformed, but she looked happy: a young woman having fun at camp.

There were books, too, and a big green binder was open. A vase held autumn leaves beside a pot of freesia.

A white-haired woman of about forty was striding to the front, looking at notes.

"Sisters, brothers, friends, I want to thank you all for coming to our celebration of Helena's life..."

The program said the white-haired woman's name was Miranda Detson-White and her tone was sad but strong as she spoke to the hushed audience.

Helena Jessica Quintham had been born in Orillia in 1972 to Mary Stone-Quintham and her partner, Wilbur Quintham. There were two other children. Helena enjoyed the outdoors, canoeing and hiking. She wrote poems and wanted to go to university, but attended business classes instead because of societal and familial expectations.

Helena's spirit remained free while she worked at traditional office jobs in small towns, but that spirit was killed when she suffered rape and harassment. Powerless and dispirited, suffering and aching, she had found healing at the Centre before she was murdered.

Helena was a victim of patriarchy and abuse of power, but she was also a survivor.

Beside me, the baby whimpered.

"And now I'd like to read a poem by Alice Goodley."

My friend
of the northern woods
I embrace you
cradle
your great free spirit
in the wind
untaken by your assassin.
The powerful who
stole your body
raped destroyed
left this.

Jane would later scoff at the "improvised service," but I found it moving. Miranda played the guitar and another woman sang "Blowing in the Wind." The underlying theme was anger at the injustice done to Helena, the senseless killing, the victimization of a patriarchal society, but good memories were mentioned, too. Someone talked about the hilarious hall-painting party Helena had been part of.

An older woman spoke about Helena's plans to take university courses and her hopes of going to England.

And then there were childhood stories haltingly related by a woman who turned out to be Helena's mother, Mary. She seemed dazed, sedated perhaps, and uncomfortable, obviously not used to speaking in public. She wore a green suit and red lipstick, but her face looked swollen from crying. Everyone listened politely while she talked about Helena being "a good little helper around the house," a conscientious student, a happy girl who enjoyed birthday parties and playing Monopoly and checkers...

She began to weep, and a woman came forward and embraced her. The young mother beside me wiped away a tear.

Miranda played the guitar again. I was surprised to hear "Amazing Grace."

"Mary requested this," Miranda said quietly.

The service was followed by tea and muffins and what would have been called fellowship anywhere else. I carried my mug to the front— Jane behind me— to look at the items on the pine table.

Close up, the photos showed an entirely unremarkable woman with a round face. She wasn't pretty and she wasn't ugly: she was the kind of person you would pass on the street and not notice. A traditional high-school graduation picture showed a young woman who smiled broadly, and she sparkled in the canoeing picture— paddle raised in a salute, trees in the distance, but there was something grave about her in the other pictures, even when she was smiling. She was a person who took herself seriously. She reminded me somehow of her mother, Mary, talking at the service.

There Helena was, at ten or eleven, in her pyjamas by a wrapping-paper strewn Christmas tree. There was the birthday child wearing a paper hat. And there was Helena crouched on a braided rug beside a black kitten. There she was at the painting party someone had mentioned. She seemed out-of-place. She wasn't hugging or sticking her tongue out or holding a paint brush over someone's head. She stood apart, looking distant and aloof.

The binder held poems. Rhymed, sentimental verse.

I remember my kitten
Never gave her a lickin'

The blue lake in my mind
Was always kind.

And—

I have discovered my soul
Now I am whole.
Free as the breeze
No longer to freeze.

There were also postcards, Hallmark birthday cards, and theatre stubs. She had seen *Titanic* and *Fargo*. There was a thank-you card from someone called Muriel ("I'll never forget your kindness" was written in black ink) and an invitation to a potluck at the Women's House. A brochure for a charter trip to England was tucked into the back.

The books included *Women Who Run with the Wolves*, *Pulling Your Own Strings* and *Far from the Madding Crowd*. *Wolves* looked new and unread, but the Hardy paperback was worn and thumbed. And no wonder: it was a cancelled library book.

Bits and pieces of an unremarkable life.

Jane kept peering at the photos and shaking her head.

"The poetry's..." Not very good, I was going to add, but Helena's mother was suddenly standing beside me, shifting her handbag from hand to hand.

"I was reading your daughter's poems," I said.

Mary nodded. She had bought Helena a rhyming dictionary when she was fourteen, she said.

"She should have written for greeting cards," Mary added. "I always said so." She glanced at Jane. "Were you friends of Helena's?"

"Friends of friends," I said quickly.

"So many people. I never would have guessed she knew so many people. We're having a regular funeral but Miranda said I should come to this. She arranged a drive for me and everything."

"Don't you live in Toronto?"

"No, we're up by Huntsville."

Her tears had dried. Close up, she was prettier than Helena had been, with a smooth white complexion— despite the puffiness from crying— and dark crisp hair. But like her daughter, she wore thick glasses, and she was also chubby. Her green suit was too tight.

"I wish Wilbur was here, but..." She didn't finish, but pointed to the Christmas picture. "That's his slippers in the corner. You can just make them out. He's not in a lot of pictures 'cause he always took them, but I took this one. He just can't get over what happened."

I expressed my sympathy.

Suddenly a woman screamed.

"I'm so FUCKING sick of this world! It makes me really puking sick! FUCK THE POLICE! FUCK ALL MEN!"

Sobs and cries filled the air.

The woman who had screamed was on the floor, holding her shoulders and rocking back and forth. Another woman knelt beside her, comforting, but the woman kept crying.

Jane put her teacup down on the pine table and marched out.

"If you ask me, they hardly knew Helena," Jane said.

We were in the first coffee shop we had come to, a white-tiled bagel place. Jane had rushed past the cameraman, covering her face.

"That's why they had to drag her poor mother here. They didn't know the first thing about Helena!"

"She went to the women's centre, though. There was a picture of her helping to paint the hall."

"Yeah. A lot of women probably go there, but so what? She's just a victim to them, a woman who's somebody because she was raped. Or so they say!"

"And killed," I said.

"But not by Neil. They've got it wrapped up in this tidy package. Brutal cop rapes her then kills her because she's pressed charges. They've already convicted Neil. They're judge and jury combined. Neil never raped that woman. Never in a million years."

"You know I don't believe he's guilty, either. But it was sad seeing her pathetic pictures, and the sentimental girlish verses in the binder. They cared enough to put on the service."

"As a political act! You know what I think? I think they— someone there— got her believing she was raped. That's what I think! They all see themselves as victims! That woman screaming, 'Fuck this, fuck that.' It made me sick. 'Fuck all men!' That about sums it up.

"And subjecting her mother to all that bullshit!"

Jane jumped up and tried to pull her coat on, but the sleeve was tangled. "Fuck, fuck!" Her voice shook as she struggled into her coat.

"All this political stuff drives me crazy! Those women don't know the first thing about Neil! Talk about prejudice!"

"Maybe..." Maybe you shouldn't have come, I was going to say, but tears began running down Jane's cheeks.

She dug into her purse, threw some coins onto the table, and flounced out.

The cameraman had been joined by two others and Miranda was being interviewed when I got back to the Women's House.

"It's a sad time for all of us," Miranda said. "Helena was our friend, our sister, and we mourn her. What happened to her should never happen to a human being."

Inside, they were collecting mugs and plates. The woman who had screamed was gone, but Mary Quintham was following another woman down the steps at the side of the hall.

The basement had obviously once housed the Sunday school. The faded green walls could have used a coat of paint, and you could see where Bible posters had hung. The orange floor tiles were scuffed. A few folding chairs stood near a stage draped with dusty beige curtains.

I almost bumped into a grey-haired woman carrying an empty tray as she bustled out of what was obviously the kitchen, but she assumed I was looking for the ladies' room. "It's to the right of the stage." She nodded in that direction and gave me a harried smile.

The word "Ladies" had been painted over with an X. Someone had used markers to draw yellow and red balloons on a piece of bristol board and written, in blue: "There ain't no Ladies here."

A door was open across the narrow hall.

"...I'll be fine. There's no need to worry." Helena's mother's voice.

"It's your safety we're concerned about. We can put you up. We'd be glad to."

There were steps on the stairs. I put my hand on the balloon sign, ready to push the door open.

"—what she said. He blamed..."

"I know how you feel. Believe me. I've heard it all before and..."

The footsteps came closer. I pushed the washroom door open and ducked into one of the two stalls. Just in time. Two women entered. One went into the other stall.

"So is her mother going home or what?"

"Angie's talking to her in the office." I recognized Miranda's voice.

"Beast. At least she came. I don't know why any woman would go back to someone like that." The toilet flushed. "Issuing ultimatums like some potentate." Clothes being adjusted. "What the hell's there for her to go back to? You tell me. Saying she wasn't to come to the service here or else!"

The women changed places.

"Another victim," the second woman muttered as she washed her hands.

The door to the hall jerked open as I came out of my cubicle.

"You won't believe it!" The new woman— Angie?— was flushed. There were tears on her cheeks. She was the woman who had been on television. She wore a long tent-like denim dress and Birkenstocks over thick socks. "She left! Helena's mother's gone. Says she'll take a bus home!"

"You let her go?" Miranda yelled. "What were you doing?" She jumped out of the stall.

"I couldn't stop her! She started crying and then she was out of the door. I called to her—"

"Fuck!"

Miranda shot out the door and down the hall. The other two women ran after her. No one took any notice of me.

I told myself I had an advantage over Miranda and her friends: a car. Toronto's efficient subway system and the parking problem made it much easier to leave cars at home. Travelling by bus and subway also was better for the environment, and that would be a consideration for Miranda and company, I thought as I drove to the Greyhound terminal downtown.

The problem was that Mary Quintham never showed up. Even if she didn't know the route, someone, a kindly ticket agent, would have told her. She could have taken a taxi.

I waited two hours and drove home.

There was no answer at Bron's, and after calling the Humane Society (no Willy there) and eating heated up cream of cauliflower soup, I got out my notebook and found myself writing about Mary Quintham.

I could see, suddenly, her kitchen: the pot-holders, the silver bread box and matching canister set on the polished counter, the plaque reading "No matter where I feed my guests, it seems they like my kitchen best"; her big purse set on the table.

Near Huntsville, she had said, and I was just going to call Peter to see if he could access the Huntsville telephone directory when the phone rang.

It was Robert Browning.

"What is the saying? 'Discretion is the better part of valour,'" he said after we had exchanged pleasantries (and he'd seen me on the news in a restaurant— I hadn't turned the television on). "I did indeed show the picture of your friend around but, alas, only the young fellow who works the afternoon shift on the front desk recalled a man in a windbreaker with a curly-haired woman. He was not sure, however, and made the point of saying he couldn't swear to it."

"What colour hair? Did he say?"

"He wasn't sure. Frizzy hair, curly hair. That's all I could learn. And she wore a dark coat."

"So he saw them together in the lobby?"

"In the Mozart Lounge, where we met so fortuitously. His name is Paulo. He was delivering a message that had come to the desk. I know the church, by the way, where the service was held."

"It's not a church any more. It's a women's centre, called the Women's House."

"Dear me. It used to be a Baptist church. I went to school with the pastor. That was William Dicks. I wonder whatever happened to him. Quite the limp he had, from polio..."

Robert went on about his old friend for a while.

Then: "But the surprising thing was that I recognized one of his parishioners, a Mrs. Dalby, on television. My oh my. She ran the show, organizing suppers and what have you. One of those well-meaning but rather frightening women who boss the minister around. She must be liberated now."

"Sounds like she was always liberated."

"Right on. Shall I look her up? Do some sleuthing? She'd remember me, I'm sure. She arranged a debate about having teen dances and so on in the church basement. She was for the dances, but others were against. It's only a hop, skip and a jump from the Quartet to her neighbourhood."

"Sleuth away."

Before he hung up, Robert relayed greetings from Jake, who hoped my writing was going well.

Finally, there was an answer at Bron's.

Maureen.

Who had seen me on television.

"What're you trying to do? It's none of your business! Stay out of our affairs!"

Chapter Eighteen

Telephone directories at the Guelph Library revealed that the Quinthams lived in Beaver Falls, ten miles before Huntsville. I would call on Helena's parents on Saturday, when I drove to Meredith to pick up Peter.

I didn't get much writing done. I had to fill in at the store for Peter, and The Bookworm was busy with customers looking for new fall titles.

Bron didn't attend the class Thursday night. I phoned and phoned Neil's number, but no one answered, and when I drove by the house, the drapes were pulled tight and Maureen's car wasn't there.

"I've known women like Maureen," Amanda said at the Walper

Hotel after the class. "Capable and efficient, but always on their guard. They hate it when anyone invades or threatens their territory. The bank was full of them. Rising executives. Big executives."

"I just wish I could speak to Bron. She must have gone to Toronto with Maureen after all."

"Poor woman."

"It's too bad they couldn't have a better relationship."

"Maybe she resents her mother. Who knows what went on?"

I didn't say anything. I hadn't told her yet about Bron's drinking problem.

"Not that I'm suggesting Bron was like my mother, but things fester. I should know. It was a good class tonight, wasn't it? As soon as Bella said about that aunt being a space alien I thought: wow!"

Roberta had described a fussy old aunt with good, concrete detail ("Show, don't tell") and Bella had come up with the idea of the aunt really being from outer space.

"You could do something with that. Prim old fuddy-duddy aunt gets this weird notion. It wouldn't have to be a spaceship. It could be anything. She could think someone was following her. Suddenly, out of the blue.

"Look who just walked in."

Our future bestselling author in his pseudo-hunting jacket and a blonde woman were standing in the doorway.

"There's the creature who banished Marilyn," Amanda whispered as she waved Brad over.

His wife's name was Charlene. She wore designer jeans and a white sweater with nautical designs. She thought Brad's work was "terrific. I just hope no one steals his idea."

I didn't like Charlene, who believed Brad would sell his book for "megabucks" as soon as it was finished. She quizzed me thoroughly about my knowledge of agents and publishers.

"Writing's like anything. It's who you know," she said. "Brad should be networking more."

Charlene was designing a web page for Brad. And did I know anyone in New York? Hollywood? Kitchener was the boonies. She missed Toronto, although that wasn't where the writing action really was either, was it? And would there be any editors at the retreat?

"Brad's too good for Canada," she said, putting a pink-nailed hand on his arm.

She ignored Amanda after Amanda said she hadn't published yet.

Brad glowed at his wife's praise, which flowed on. And on. Charlene reminded me, in a way, of Jane, although Jane was less naive. Charlene was a loans officer at a bank and I thought I wouldn't want to sit on the opposite side of her desk.

I wasn't sad when Amanda said she should be off. "Morning comes early. I'm on a roll and I want to be at the computer by nine."

"I'd better be going, too. Get my beauty rest. I have to be at the store tomorrow and the day after that I have a long drive north."

Charlene said, "Oh, I thought you wrote full time."

Amanda and I were still giggling when we parted in the parking lot on Charles Street. She handed me a thick manila envelope.

"Hollywood, here you come," I said, holding up her stories.

Chapter Nineteen

I had two surprises.

The first was that the letter I received from Suzanne Maloff on the Friday before I went to Meredith was not only literate, but written in an elegant, sloping handwriting.

Dear Miss Archer, [Miss Archer— after she had beaten me up!]

You'll be surprised to hear from me.

I know my son, Burton, did not kill his grandmother. You may think a mother would stick up for her child, but I have been visiting Burton at the detention centre and I have information which will be of interest to your friend. Burton's lawyer is no good to talk to.

Can we meet? If next Tuesday at 2 at the food court at Stone Road Mall is agreeable, please leave a message at the number at the end of this letter.

There will be no trouble at the mall, please believe me.

Yours sincerely,

(Mrs.) Suzanne Maloff

That was the first surprise. I phoned the number and said I would meet Suzanne on Tuesday.

The second surprise was that Helena's father looked like a skinnier version of my publisher, Jake Hendricks— the same dark hair, the sort of brooding features I associated with composers and artists, and he was a draft dodger!

Finding their place wasn't hard. The population of Beaver Falls looked to be about four hundred. It was more a hamlet than a village, a sleepy crossing of two dusty roads. A large weathered sign, near the highway cut-off, advertised "Beaver Falls Canoes." But the clapboard factory was boarded up. There was an old brick church with a fenced cemetery (was Helena buried there?) and the only other place of note was Hank's Service Centre, a gas bar/restaurant/general store filled with guys in billed caps and women in jeans and windbreakers who were drinking coffee and passing the time of day.

These good folks were glad to give me directions, but they were less eager to talk about Wilbur Quintham, except to say— he was a draft dodger! From New York!

But there were raised eyebrows and meaningful looks and I was pretty sure I heard the words "son of a bitch." Yes, it was terrible what had happened to Helena. A woman in a quilted jacket who was buying a case of pop said, "You never know, do you? Her poor mother."

"You must be a friend of Helena's," she added.

I let her think so.

"He wasn't going to have a minister, but old Reverend Smith took the service. Mary used to teach Sunday school, but none of them went to church. Reverend Smith was her pastor one time."

"I attended the memorial service in Toronto," I said. Now they were all listening. The girl at the cash register stared at me. "Helena had a lot of friends in the city. Her mother was there, too."

"Some woman came and got her," the girl on cash said. Her ears were filled with studs. She looked about eighteen. "That's what I heard, anyway."

"It was a lovely service," I said. "Very moving. Some of her friends spoke and a woman played a guitar."

"That's what they do these days, I guess," the pop woman said.

"Lots of churches have the guitar," the cash girl said.

Guitar versus non-guitar talk went on for a while.

"Well, I don't know. I prefer a choir myself," the older woman said. "Guess I'm just plain old-fashioned. You must be from Toronto, too."

"Near Toronto."

The woman shook her head as if she felt sorry for me.

"Helena used to work here," the cashier said. "Before my time."

"Here? In this very place? She never mentioned it."

"She was just a kid," the older woman said.

"I heard she got fired," the cashier said.

"Well, it's easy to mess a cash register up," I said. "I've made a mistake or two myself in my husband's book- store. I'd probably get fired, too."

"There's nothing to it," the cashier said. "I just hate it when the credit cards don't go through. You got to wait and wait and you've got a line-up and everyone's hollering. And one time someone gave me a fake hundred-dollar bill."

She twittered on about cashier work, not telling me why Helena had been fired.

The older woman wasn't saying, either.

"So you're going to call on the family?"

"I'm driving north anyway and I thought I'd stop. I felt so sorry for Mary in Toronto."

"You can bet he won't have the welcome mat out," the woman said.

She was right.

The man swinging the axe was slight, and although he was working vigorously, there was a defeated look about the shoulders. It was a crisp, sunny day. His red jacket was outlined against the pine trees behind him. The air was pungent with fall. Maples blazed across the road and in front of the house.

He probably did not hear my car, but he straightened up when he saw me and put the axe down. And there, surprise, surprise, was the face like Jake's. He wore old-fashioned granny glasses, and there was, too, a hint of John Lennon about him.

But I was romanticizing. He was not glad to see me.

The axe dropped when I introduced myself. He didn't recognize my name. I found myself feeling surprised, let down. He looked like a reader and I knew I had used my real name on the assumption that he would see me as a kindred spirit. We're both from the States; my ex had escaped the draft, too. We had both come north, to Canada. We were of the same generation. Like me, he had probably loved the Rolling Stones, Dylan. We would have read the same books then: Richard Brautigan, Tom Wolfe... Bosom buddies: he'd tell me all.

"I hope you're not with the press," he said.

"I'm not with anyone. I met your wife at the Women's House in Toronto."

He waited.

"I'm on my way north... I mean, I was passing by and I thought I'd drop by and express my sympathy. Helena was a lovely young woman."

He picked up the axe. I stepped back. He went back to chopping wood. His actions had an angrier edge; finally, he threw the axe violently away.

I looked at the house. He noticed and said he wasn't asking me in. His wife was in a bad way.

"Look, I don't know what you want or why you came. We're not talking to anyone, not to the press, not to lawyers, not to snoopers. Why don't you leave? We just buried her. I don't know you and you don't know me. It's all crap. Nothing but crap. Leave us alone."

"I'm—"

"I'll walk you to your car. I think I want you to get out of here."

"Didn't you want your wife to go to the memorial service in Toronto?"

"Car!" He motioned to the Volvo. Conrad was practically having convulsions behind the glass. I had to reprimand him sharply or he would have been out in a flash. He had never bitten anyone, but he hated angry faces.

"Why don't you mind your own business? All of you've caused enough trouble."

"I'm sorry." I shut the door between Conrad and the man.

"I don't know what you're talking about."

"Sure. Get out of here! And tell Tatiana not to bother us any more. Tell her to stay away, too."

"I don't know anyone named Tatiana. Is that who drove your wife home from Toronto?"

"If I see her again—"

"—what? You'll commit an axe murder? They said at the service centre that you were a draft dodger. I guess all that idealism about peace has flown out of the window," I said.

"Go to hell," he said, and walked to the house.

I used the pay phone at the service centre to call the Quartet. Robert wasn't in his room, but I left a message that I would call him that night. He could ask that church woman he knew if she knew "Tatiana."

I ordered coffee in the restaurant. The coffee drinkers had thinned out, but I recognized a few faces from earlier. A chubby young woman in a pink jacket raised an enquiring eyebrow. Everyone must have heard about me by now. I shook my head.

"It's a terrible thing," she told me. "Helena was a few years older 'n me, but I'm telling you, it really hits home when it's someone you know. Like, you hear about stuff happening all the time, but you never think it'll happen to someone you know. It doesn't seem real. I still can't believe it."

She had a rosy, guileless face. Her old-fashioned engagement and wedding bands cut into her fingers. She was eating fries.

"Did you know her long?"

"A while," I lied. "I was going to Meredith anyway and it's not far out of the way."

"I got a cousin in Meredith."

"My father-in-law was the Chief of Police up there until he retired. They have a bed and breakfast now. He had a heart attack."

"You don't say! My cousin'll know him."

"Hugh Hall."

"Jeez. How about that? Is he okay?"

"He's fine. My husband stayed up for a while. I'm picking him up."

"You from Toronto?"

"Guelph."

"Never been there. Did you see Mary?"

"Just her husband."

"She's pretty bad. She couldn't stop crying at the reception after the funeral. The women put it on in the church. They do it for everyone. They weren't churchgoers, but Mary used to teach Sunday school and old Reverend Smith looked after it. Wilbur's an atheist."

"Is he?" The waitress brought my coffee and refilled my neighbour's cup.

"One of them draft dodgers. Used to grow dope. This isn't gossip because he got busted. Anyone can tell you. They say his family has money, down in the States, New York or somewhere."

"So Mary was from around here?"

"Just down the road. They built on her grandfather's land. She lived with him first and, boy, I guess that caused a ruckus. Back in the good old days, you know? He was this long-haired hippie who got busted and Mary takes up with him! He was living in this van he had. Before my time, but I've heard all about it."

"He doesn't have long hair any more."

"Nope. But he's a vegetarian and he's got his land posted— he doesn't allow hunting on it. He bought this woodlot and doesn't allow hunting.

One time he fired off shots after someone. Writing letters to the papers about how hunting's redneck and cruel, like deer are people and have the same feelings as us!"

"He fired a gun? At people?"

"Not directly at them, but in the air like. Didn't try to hide it or nothing. Said, 'How does it feel?'"

"Did they call the police?"

"Huh." She rolled her eyes and leaned forward to whisper. "Pretty hard to do, considering they were..." She mouthed something and looked around the room. "Jacking," she whispered in my ear.

"If he's against hunting why would he have a gun?"

"Shotgun. It was a shotgun."

"For bears," I suggested.

"A shotgun? You generally use a rifle for bears. And my brother-in-law's cousin set rabbit snares once— wasn't even on Wilbur's land, but back of his woodlot, and the snares mysteriously disappeared. Wilbur'd be one of those guys who throw paint on fur coats if he lived in Toronto."

"I guess people don't wear fur coats here."

"Some of 'em, the older ones. But he'd know that was going too far. I don't know what he thinks the Indians lived off of. If you don't shoot some deer, all the deer'll starve. Everyone knows that. Jack goes to camp in the fall and he generally gets his deer."

People hunted around Meredith, too. Once we dropped in on Allison when she was packaging venison for the freezer. She gave us a roast and steak and Peter actually looked forward to eating it. Hugh wasn't much of a hunter, but there was always venison in the fall, either from Joe or from one of Hugh's buddies.

The locals here would find Wilbur hard to understand. Even Marion, who said men leaving for camp in the fall was like overgrown boys going to play He-man, made no fuss over gifts of venison.

"I've had venison," I said. "In Meredith."

"Good. Mmm. Especially if it's not from a big old buck. The gamey stuff's not so good, but Jack doesn't care."

"Jack's your husband?"

"He's the one! My own and only! We've been married five years now."

Jack repaired televisions and was getting into computers. Jack didn't like his venison "gussied up," and one time she made this dish with wine and mushrooms and ended up throwing it out...

"Mary grew up with hunting," I said, steering the conversation.

"She sure did! People feel sorry for her. I don't know how she puts up with him myself. But to each his own..."

"I heard Helena used to work here when she was a teenager," I said. "I was surprised she never mentioned it."

"I was just a kid myself, but yeah, she worked here. Just one summer. You should see this place in the summer, packed with tourists. You wouldn't catch me working here summers. You must of gone to that service they had in Toronto?" But it was not quite a question. She had heard about me, because she didn't stop. "It was on the news. Good thing we have a satellite dish or I don't know what we'd do."

"It was very moving. She had a lot of friends in Toronto. Everyone liked her so much."

There was no response to this.

"I guess you didn't get to meet any of her Toronto friends," I ventured. "She never mentioned bringing anyone here."

"One time she did," a man's voice from two tables down said.

"Well, I never met her." My friend wasn't startled by the interruption.

"One of the libbers." The man turned around. He was fiftyish, with a ruddy face. "Skinny woman with no make-up. Nothing to write home about."

"Who'd look at you anyways?" my companion shot back. She moved to my table. "You don't mind, do you? I'm Judy, by the way."

"Carolyn."

Judy plunked what was left of her fries onto my table, reached into a large plastic bag and took out her cigarettes. "Okay if I smoke?"

I nodded.

"I've got to quit, I know. I never met her friend from Toronto. Boy, she sure changed. I can tell you that much. I don't know what happened, but she'd come home and pass you on the street and not say hi. It was like she didn't know you and I'm not the only one that happened to."

"That doesn't sound like Helena," I said.

"She got to be just like her father, that's what everyone said. I know you shouldn't talk bad about the dead, but it was suddenly like she was too good for everyone here."

"This was after she moved to Toronto?"

"Yeah. She was in Leicester first and if you ask me she was happier there. She came home with this little red Honda. Secondhand, but she was pleased as punch. Drove me to Huntsville once when I had a doctor's appointment. Friendly as all-get-out, and later we went for coffee. She looked good, too; lost some weight and I kinda think she had a boyfriend."

"She never had one here?"

"Nope. Not that she didn't try. That summer she worked here, she'd get all dolled up with make-up— Mary sold Avon— and sit right down with the men customers. Sit at their table! Poor thing didn't know they were making fun of her. And she wore this hairnet thing with sequins all over it, like an old lady would wear."

"I heard she got fired."

"Yeah, poor girl. Butch— he owned this place then— just couldn't get her to wait on customers. She'd sit with the guys and tell them about her rich relatives in New York. And everyone else would be hollering for their orders. I guess finally Butch had enough. Her father came and complained."

"Did he?"

"He was gonna sue, he said, and called Butch all kinds of names. Said Helena was too good for them."

"What does he do, anyway?"

"Well! He makes yogurt, sells it to health stores. And he buys old cars and fixes 'em up and sells 'em. He's in one of those car-auction places. And they say his folks send him money."

"None of them came for the funeral?"

"Not that I know of. Maybe they send him money to keep away.

Helena said once she went down there, and told all these stories about their mansions and swimming pools, but it turned out she made it up. Mary said she never went. I shouldn't be talking about her like this."

"I know she had a vivid imagination," I said. "Sometimes I think... I wonder... if... I shouldn't be talking like this, either. But... I don't know. I wonder if she really was raped." I was feeling my way.

Judy ate her last fry.

"She hinted her boyfriend was a cop," Judy said. "She didn't come right out and say it, but that was just like Helena."

"Are her brothers like her?"

"They're... different. Jimmy went down south to college but he quit and got a job with the post office. He's near Kingston. Harry's up near Thunder Bay. They're all right, I guess, but, I don't know. They were sure different, all right. They never joined in. Like, all the boys play hockey, but not them. Mary's friendly, and if she has complaints she keeps them to herself, but it's not like it would be if she hadn't married him. It's like, they didn't know how to act normal. Like Helena with that hairnet. They never socialized.

"And they never had stuff like other kids. One time, Harry went on a school trip and they were supposed to bring sleeping bags but he had a blanket roll! All their clothes came from the bargain basement, but it's not like they didn't have money. Helena'd wear these cheap stretchy pants when the other girls had Levis."

"Weird."

"You said it. She spruced up for a while when she worked in Leicester, but it was downhill once she got to Toronto. No more make-up, and she gained all her weight back and then some. I should talk. I'm supposed to be on a diet and my hubby would kill me if he saw me eating these fries. And speaking of him—" she looked at her watch. "He's supposed to pick me up at one. He went over to his mother's to get the tires for the truck. We got to go into Huntsville to buy groceries. They charge an arm and a leg here. It's highway robbery."

"It's good to talk to someone who knew Helena so well when she was younger," I said.

It was almost supper time when I reached Meredith. I'd stopped in a park to let Conrad do his stuff, but mostly I'd driven slowly, thinking about this strange person who was Helena. A strange girl who didn't fit in, a girl with a father who was different and seen as odd in the small community. A girl who embroidered and fabricated and wanted male attention. A girl who was so witless she didn't see when guys were laughing at her. A girl whose father embarrassed her, whose values wouldn't allow buying appropriate clothing. A father who probably thought he had embraced the down-to-earth, back-to-the-land way of life without understanding the first thing about living in a small place. Or about living, period. A father like that would produce a daughter with an inferiority complex.

A girl who never had a date, or a boyfriend.

And then she was a woman who fantasized about an OPP officer...

And a young woman who felt out of place at the Women's House.

And who was Tatiana?

Was Tatiana someone who could have had access to Neil's revolver? And why? Why would this woman want to harm Neil?

No, it had to be someone who knew him well.

Someone who knew about Helena.

There was only one such person.

Jane.

I had only her word that she hadn't found Helena's name in the trust company's computer. Helena struck me as a sensible woman where finances were concerned. She had worked to buy herself a car (the red Honda) and it was reasonable to think she purchased RRSPs. Maybe she had money from her father's family and that was invested.

And if Jane had found out where Helena lived, it would have been easy to tail her.

Jane had smarts. She could have bribed someone at the Quartet—she was familiar with the hotel, her clients stayed there— for the key to Neil's room. After bribing a prostitute to doctor his drink.

Jane would know about escort services.

But it might have been even simpler. Maybe Jane was the one

drinking with Neil at the hotel. In a wig, no one would have recognized her— none of the overseas clients.

What was it she had said? "I can think of better places to spend my time than a smokey bar." Something like that... She seemed to know what the Mozart Lounge was like...

But wouldn't Neil have remembered if Jane was with him at the hotel?

But according to Bron, he didn't remember much.

Or, Jane paid a hooker to doctor Neil's drink and then Jane followed Neil to his room, went in and took his revolver— or got it from his car— and followed Helena and killed her.

She didn't have much time to find Helena, but it would have taken only seconds to get the information from the computer.

And Jane had overreacted to what went on at the memorial service. She had protested too much.

Or felt guilty? Afraid? Is that why she'd run off?

And Jane had been testy when Bron asked if she'd heard from Neil again that day. "If he left a message, I never received it."

And— the car swerved again— *Suzanne Maloff knew Jane.*

Could Suzanne's information have to do with Jane? Did she know of some old grievance, some complicated story?

But why would Jane want to hurt Neil?

Questions, questions! They were temporarily forgotten as Peter hugged me. He had been worried about me, he said. He had phoned The Bookworm, Emma, Scottie, but no one knew what time I had left Guelph.

This worry was new for him. He was still holding my hand when we sat down to eat Marion's chick-pea and chicken casserole (flavoured with lemon and rosemary). A new regime! Marion informed me. Healthy and light from now on, no matter what Hugh said.

Hugh was resting upstairs. He was fine, fine. But they would be going to London for more tests. In case Hugh needed by-pass surgery.

"They claim you're as good as new once you have by-pass," Peter said. "It's nothing these days. They do them all the time. Allison says the same thing."

"Where is Doctor Allison this weekend? I thought she'd be here," I said.

"She was here last weekend. She's taken the boys to Kingston," Marion said.

"To the trailer they have?" In the pen, I wanted to add, but didn't.

"They're in a motel. And it's just for today. They left after school on Friday and will be home tonight." Marion didn't look pleased. "She has to study."

No one spoke for a while.

"It's a trip for the boys anyway," I said lamely.

"A long and tiring trip," Marion said. "But what's the good of worrying? If there's one good thing that's come from Hugh's heart attack it's the realization that worrying does not benefit anyone."

"You never struck me as a worrier, Marion."

"I've worried about Hugh. He hasn't been well. And I'm worried about Allison. And the boys? What kind of future will they have with Steven?"

"At least you don't have to worry about us," Peter told his mother.

After dinner, and after saying hello to Hugh, who was paler, a few pounds thinner, but his usual gruff, affectionate self, Peter and I drove to the lodge so I could finalize plans for the retreat.

"I have so much to tell you," I said in the car.

"What?"

"The memorial service. Yes, don't make a face. I did go. With Jane, Neil's former live-in. Suzanne Maloff wants to see me on Tuesday. And I stopped off today to see Helena's father. And Maureen told me to stay out of their business! Did you see me on TV? I didn't see it myself, but I guess the camera caught me because Maureen saw my gorgeous face."

"I've been doing a lot of walking. And a lot of puttering around in Mom's car. There's something I want to talk to you about, too," Peter said.

"What?"

"Later, later. We'll stop at the hotel after we see Bill and Linda, okay?"

"Tell me now!"

"It'll take too long. Anyway, we're here. The lodge, m'dear!"

I always felt happy when I visited Bill and Linda Johannsen's lodge. Their taste and the joy they felt for life had transformed the old, dark hunting lodge into a place filled with light and beautiful things— Linda's artwork, Bill's carvings, the pine furniture, the quilts on the walls.

But it was their gracious and very real and happy sincerity that had made the lodge prosper. Tourists came from here and from the States, Europe, Japan. They told their friends who told their friends and the rest, as they say, was history. We always spent New Year's Eve at their place and Bill and Linda visited back and forth with Peter's parents.

Big smiles were on their fair, Scandinavian faces— I couldn't recall an occasion when they had looked gloomy— and there were hugs and kisses all around. Linda wore a beaded vest. Her dress style was as creative as the decor.

"We've got a houseful," she said, "so let's go into the penthouse." She meant their private quarters. "But first you have to see the gift shop."

"Shop spelled shoppe," Bill quipped. "I never thought we'd have a shoppe, but c'est la vie. And first they need refreshments. Cocoa? Tea? Hot rum toddies?"

"Toddies, I think," Linda said, "on this cool and darkening night.

"We have books in the shop, too," she added to me. "And magazines, the best magazines, none of this supermarket stuff. We'll educate the tourists yet."

"Great for the retreat, too. I gather you're talking literary mags?"

"The same," she said over her shoulder as she led the way to "the penthouse."

"A lot of the students had no idea that creatures like literary magazines existed until they came to my class."

I loved their apartment. It was new, added just the year before. The word "penthouse" was not inappropriate because the main room had a cathedral ceiling. One wall was glass and faced the lake. Upstairs, an open gallery led to two large bedrooms and a study area. Everything was light wood with bright splashes of colour, red and magenta, in the artwork.

"You don't have to worry about a thing," Linda said when we had our drinks. "I'll give you the east wing— two to a room, unless someone wants to pay extra for a single in the west wing. And for writing, you can use the old cabins down by the lake— the fireplaces work, but there are no showers, as you know— or the carriage house."

"And don't forget the great outdoors," Bill said. "Cold but good for reflection, no? And for human inspiration, your people are welcome to write in the main lounge."

"And I thought you could come here for meetings," Linda said. "Unless you want to use the small dining room, but that's so dark. Meals from the menu, except for the dinner Saturday night and we'll talk about that. I've written down some suggestions."

"It sounds wonderful. I'm really looking forward to it now."

"Now?" Linda asked.

"I've been too busy. Too much happening."

I wasn't going to discuss Neil with them. And suddenly, in this happy place, I did not want to talk about him. Or about Helena.

We chatted a while, mainly about Hugh, and then we inspected the gift shop, which was practically a bookstore! Selected titles only, please! Gift coffee-table books were there, but I was pleased to see a variety of Canadian titles, many of them by regional presses. And the magazines!

The rest of the space— half of it— was filled with prints, handmade sweaters, woven tablecloths and hangings, and locally made pottery. Not a "Canada" coffee mug in sight, or anything stamped "Meredith."

"We'll have to come back and browse when we have more time," Peter said.

"Come back nothing," I said, and selected a handful of magazines.

Half an hour later, sitting over the awful draft beer which they serve at the Meredith Hotel, Peter told me his news.

He wanted to move back to Meredith.

He wanted to buy the lodge. Bill and Linda planned to return to Minnesota to be closer to their grown-up children.

What did I think?

Chapter Twenty

Peter was in his forties, and what had he accomplished? Nothing but owning The Bookworm, and that was going nowhere. I had published books and would go on writing and publishing. Next to me, he was a zero.

He was tired of The Bookworm ("I can see myself there at sixty-five.") and the solitary time up north had made him realize he was sick of southern Ontario, of Guelph, of all small cities. He was even tired of our little stone house. He was tired of being crowded, of every day being the same as the one before and the one after.

He knew he wanted the lodge as soon as Marion mentioned that Linda and Bill were looking for a buyer. Maybe he didn't exactly love Meredith itself, but the world would come to our door. Every day would be different. He would be doing something new.

And there was the outdoors. He did miss the north, the open spaces, the friendliness, the easier lifestyle.

We could sell our house and the bookstore. We could even— if I agreed, and he knew it was asking a lot— sell my grandmother's place in Maine, which I still owned and rented out.

Did I realize that the royalties from my mysteries were a lot more than the pittance he cleared at The Bookworm?

Conrad would be happier in the north.

"Of course, I wouldn't want to move if you weren't with me on this," Peter said.

"Are you sure this isn't because of your father's heart attack?"

"I guess that enters into it. I don't think they should keep the B & B— too much for Dad, too much temptation to eat rich food, to stay up too late— but Mom could help at the lodge. You'd be writing. As always."

"How does your mother feel?"

"She wants to keep the B & B going. She says it wouldn't work— her in the business, two women running things. But I'm not sure about that. They're both getting older and I'll tell you something else. Steven wants to return to Scotland when he's released. There's no future for him in Canada now, he says, but a cousin back home has offered him a job.

"So... if Allison should decide to go to Scotland with him—"

"She won't do that! And take the kids, too? Never. She's going to be a doctor. Plus, Joe wouldn't let his kids move overseas. He might even go for custody."

"You're probably right. But if she goes, and I say if, I'd want to keep a closer eye on the old folks. Allison hasn't told Mom yet, so don't say anything. That's the real reason for the blitz trip to Kingston. But I think Mom knows something is up."

Living in Meredith... the idea was so preposterous, so startling. Peter hadn't been happy growing up there, and while I had grown fond of the place, I had never considered living there.

I had never thought Peter was unhappy at The Bookworm. He owned it when I met him and I never thought of him doing anything else. It was true he was moody sometimes, a bit too quiet. But that was just the way he was. Or so I had believed.

Could it be he resented my success? I didn't think so. But I had gone on to publish novels, had become (somewhat) known, gone on book tours and all the rest of the hoopla that went along with writing popular fiction. But while this was going on, Peter was shelving books and making out Mastercard charges in the store.

But wasn't it true that I was in a slump, too? I had written recent bits and pieces, but my novel ideas had dried up. And, yes, maybe I was even tired of Guelph, of small cities. I did love the lodge. The constant comings and goings were exciting.

But too exciting for writing, perhaps?

It was a big step. Peter said that Linda and Bill would tell us if they had an offer. In the meantime, we could think about it.

But I couldn't see myself living in Meredith.

Peter talked about the lodge constantly as we drove home the next day. A new beginning, he said. Wouldn't it be wonderful? Wasn't Bill and Linda's life interesting? And there would be the great outdoors, too.

"Look at the smog!" he cried as we neared Toronto and saw a haze over the skyline. "Compare that to the northern air."

He was still talking this way when we arrived home.

I had left a cardboard box fitted with a folded towel and bowls of kibble and water on the back doorstep. The food was gone, but the box looked unused, and any cat, or a racoon, could have eaten the food.

While Peter was walking Conrad, I moved the box to the narrow flagstone pathway beside the house (where we rarely went because there was nothing much there) and left the water dish out, too.

The phone was ringing when I went inside.

It was Bron. She was in Toronto. With Bruce and Maureen. The happy couple had gone out for dinner, finally leaving Bron free to call me.

"I don't in a million years understand why I let Maureen talk me into coming with her. I guess she finally wore me down and it is easier to visit Neil... And there was the question of money, too."

"Oh, Bron. You should have come to me. I'd have lent you some."

"And how would I pay it back?"

"Never, as far as I'm concerned."

She was silent for a while.

Then she said: "Were you and Neil involved?"

"What?"

"I want to know. I may only be his ex, but I'd feel pretty foolish accepting rides from you, being buddies, and not knowing."

"Bron, we weren't involved." I said it forcefully, but my face burned. I wasn't lying. Strictly speaking, we hadn't "been involved," if by those words Bron meant had we had an affair. "Neil and I are good friends. That's all. He's a nice man, but I've never been unfaithful to Peter!"

Again, she was silent.

"Some people would be insulted by the question," I said. "Tell me what this is all about, okay?"

"It's just something Maureen said. Forget I asked. I'm sorry if I insulted you."

"What did Maureen tell you?"

"Something her father said, apparently. She thinks you're another Jane, just fooling around with Neil's head."

"Oh, for heaven's sake! Neil must have said he liked me and Maureen used that to get at you so you'd go to Toronto!"

"I didn't mean just sex," Bron said.

"I do like Neil, but... Bron, there was nothing beyond attraction."

"That's what I mean."

"Bron, I did not have an affair with Neil and I wasn't planning on having one. Ever. Let's forget this conversation happened." I took a deep breath before rushing on. "I dropped by in Beaver Falls, where Helena was from, and found out there was a lot more to Helena than met the eye. Did you know that her father was a draft dodger?"

"No, I didn't."

It was hard to tell from Bron's voice how she felt, but I forged ahead and filled her in with what I had learned. She listened without saying much. Only when I got to my suspicions about Jane did she react.

"Jane had an abortion when she was with Neil. Maureen told me all about it this weekend. Jane told her all about it. Imagine, the kid would have been Maureen's half-sister or brother! Jane said Neil wasn't crazy about starting another family and Jane wasn't sure at that point either, so she went ahead and had the abortion."

"I thought Maureen and Jane didn't get along."

"Seems like once they did. Before. Not that Maureen ever really liked her—Jane wasn't always exactly welcoming when Maureen wanted to visit, said it was 'inconvenient,' or she and Neil had plans, and they had nothing in common interest-wise, but I guess they talked. When Jane allowed Maureen to visit."

"Maybe Jane resents having had the abortion."

"She didn't seem like a woman who'd be crazy about kids."

"Have you discussed this with Neil?"

"He doesn't want to talk about it."

"So Jane having the abortion wasn't that simple. Maybe the abortion was Neil's idea."

"Maybe it was." Bron's voice was flat again. But it perked up when she said, "Maureen has been following Jane around. She was even waiting across the street from that community centre."

"The Women's House."

"Whatever."

"Then she could have seen who picked up Helena's mother. Tatiana, maybe," I said.

"She wouldn't *know* Helena's mother. She left the service early, remember? Anyway, Maureen trailed Jane when she left the coffee shop. She saw you go there, too. She didn't just see you on TV."

"So where did Jane go?"

"She went to this street called Clayburn. It's not far from where they had the service."

"And Jane didn't recognize her?"

"Maureen wore jeans and Bruce's Blue Jays cap. Plus dark glasses. Maureen's small. She would have looked like a boy."

"And then what?"

"Jane stood on the street, turned around and hailed a taxi, so Maureen lost her. But she discovered where Jane lives. Jane doesn't go to work until ten and she leaves by three. She's only working part-time. Maybe we should check her alibi, that she was in a meeting all afternoon the day Neil met her for lunch."

"It was strange she thought she had to show us her date book."

"The only trouble is, I can't see someone like Jane taking such a risk."

"Well I can," I said, "and there's something else." I told her about

Suzanne's letter. "Jane knew Suzanne. She mentioned her when we met. Maybe Suzanne's information is about Jane!"

"Maureen will be surprised about Suzanne's letter," Bron said.

"I don't think Maureen will be happy to know I'm, as she put it, getting involved."

Bron didn't say anything to this.

"Does Bruce know what Maureen is doing?" I asked.

"Are you kidding? He's already got Neil put away for life. I wouldn't be surprised if Maureen left him. What a jerk. He wants me in bed by ten-thirty. Ten-thirty comes and he looks at his watch. 'Getting sleepy, Bron?' He wants me out of the way so he can have a drink and harangue Maureen."

"So you tiptoe obediently off to bed?"

"I sat up until after midnight for spite at first. But to hell with him. I need to get away from him, too, so off I go before the prick can look at his watch. At least I can read and write in privacy."

"You're writing. Good."

"But I don't know about the retreat. I know I signed up for it, but I have a job interview tomorrow. Bruce works with someone whose mother needs a companion."

"Is a job good or bad?"

"Well, I can't be fussy, can I?"

"Why don't you simply return to Guelph? I'll pay for your retreat."

"I don't know. I'll have to see."

The front door opened. Peter and Conrad were back.

"Bron, come on the retreat. You need it."

"You're not kidding," Bron said, and then Conrad was barking and we said goodbye, but not before Bron again referred to me and Neil.

Peter and I went out for dinner. Over the garlicky lamb and cucumber salad, he told me that Linda and Bill would notify us if they had any offers for the lodge. They wanted us to have it and weren't listing the lodge with a realtor.

"We could fix up one of the cabins as a writing studio for you," Peter said.

He was still happily talking about the lodge when we went to bed at eleven-thirty.

Chapter Twenty-One

Neil phoned me in the morning. The phone rang— I reached for it— and there was Neil's voice!

"Hi there, kiddo..."

This is what had happened to Jane: she became pregnant when she was with Neil. He wasn't overjoyed, but he wasn't devastated, either. Jane was undecided. She wanted a career; she wanted children "one day." She wasn't ready to be tied down, she didn't want to live in Guelph or another small place where Neil might be transferred, and the idea of being a semi-single mother, of coping with day care, nannies, and sitters while she worked on her career— and she wanted to travel, too— didn't turn her on.

Jane decided on an abortion.

Now Jane couldn't get pregnant because of endometriosis, a condition her gynecologist suggested had been caused by earlier surgery.

The only surgery Jane had ever had was the abortion. And she had had a minor infection afterwards.

"I wanted that baby," she'd told Neil that day when she met him for lunch, "but I could tell you weren't exactly over the moon with the idea. I really wanted you to say, 'Don't have the abortion.'"

"But don't jump to conclusions," Neil said. "She was more sad than angry. Regretful, yes. According to Bron, Maureen's got Jane convicted of murdering Helena, but it's too far-fetched. I was thinking about the abortion, you know, when I was getting soused and maudlin that day and probably it's good I only got her machine."

"You called her from the hotel?"

"Yeah. I remember using the pay phone."

"But Jane said she didn't get a message from you."

"Well, machines screw up all the time. But it's no good speculating.

I've told my lawyer everything I can think of and I don't want you— or Bron— to get involved. The lawyer's already found a chambermaid who thinks she opened my door by mistake and saw me passed out around the time Helena was killed. And there were no fingerprints on the gun. Whoever used it must have wiped them off before throwing the gun away. And that's another damn thing! I wouldn't have left the gun lying around."

"You're right! Of course you're right! Someone left the gun because they wanted to frame you!"

"Looks like it to me. I hear you called on Helena's father."

"I shouldn't have done so. It was a stupid thing to do."

"Well, I had nothing to do with that, so what the heck. As I said, I don't want you to get involved, Carolyn. There could be more here than meets the eye. It could be dangerous. And be careful about Suzanne. Bron says you had a letter from her, but I think you should leave that one alone. Suzanne's nothing but trouble. She's just trying to get her son off. She's in with bikers, thugs, all kinds of criminals."

Bikers who had connections to drug dealers, I thought. Maybe Suzanne knew something about revenge for a long-ago bust...

"I want you to stay away from Suzanne," Neil said, and he sounded a lot like a cop.

After that, it was difficult to chat. I didn't want to ask Neil more about jail (he did say they were treating him well, but the food was the pits) and small talk seemed silly. He asked how I felt Bron was doing and he wanted to know if I had met Maureen. Briefly, I said. Peter was fine, Conrad was fine, my writing class was coming along. We would soon have the retreat.

"Bron should go," he said. "She needs to get away. Try to talk her into going. She'll enjoy it up there."

And so I told Neil about maybe buying the lodge, which was a neutral topic of conversation.

"Well, kiddo, if I ever get out of this one, maybe I'll call on you people for a job."

And just before we said goodbye, Neil added quietly, "I'm sorry about Bron giving you a hard time about... you know."

Of course the killer had left the gun behind to frame Neil. This was so obvious, such a sure thing, and I was still thinking about this, and the thugs Suzanne knew, when Peter called from The Bookworm.

Could I think about calling the realtor in Maine to enquire about the possibility of selling my grandmother's house? Just in case we did decide to buy the lodge?

"Just to ask about the market now," Peter said. "I know it's a big step, and I don't want you to do it if you really don't want to, but it's worth a thought. We'd have a smaller mortgage on the lodge if you sold the old place in Maine..."

It was ten-thirty. There hadn't been a single customer. He had called a local realtor to ask about selling The Bookworm.

Only to find out our situation, he stressed.

I didn't call Maine. I phoned the Quartet and reached Robert Browning. He had just gotten in.

"Wild and hairy during the week and Mother Dear on the weekends," he explained.

But he had already contacted Mrs. Dalby. She had read my books and wanted to meet me!

Was Wednesday afternoon all right?

Chapter Twenty-Two

Suzanne Maloff didn't turn up at the mall on Tuesday. I waited for two hours, called her number twice from a public phone, and each time got her machine.

I was tempted to forget it. I still hadn't read Amanda's new stories, and I could make a pot of tea... Or maybe I should call the realtor, Nicholas Pierce, in Maine, who looked after the rental of my grandmother's house. Just to see what the chances of a good sale were...

But did I want to sell my old home? It was in my name, and no matter what happened, it was there.

Instead, I checked the Guelph telephone directory. So simple! Suzanne Maloff (S. Maloff) was listed at 2310 - 3B Allenby Drive.

I had lived near Allenby Drive after Charlie and I split up. The cinder block apartment building wasn't exactly the height of luxury, and it was on the city outskirts in an area of strip malls and service centres, but my two-room apartment was a haven I decorated with plants and cheap wicker.

The trees had grown and there were video stores everywhere as well as new food take-outs, but otherwise the neighbourhood was the same. Twenty-three-ten was yellow brick, not cinder blocks, but it was very much like mine: three storeys, balconies in the front, and a parking lot at the side. The only vehicle in the lot was an old blue Honda.

The lobby had seen better days. Two mailboxes were open and the floor needed a good mopping. But an expensive racing bike sat locked by the steps and a vine wreath reading "Welcome" was on a door at the landing. The Stones were playing behind the door.

Suzanne's apartment was in the basement, four steps down. No wreath here, only scratch marks beside a new and shiny dead bolt.

I knocked on the door— there was no bell— but no one answered. A laundry room was behind her apartment, the door open. I knocked on the door of apartment 2-B— maybe this was the super, but my raps brought no response. I knocked louder and at last a thin, bearded man with reddish hair answered. His face was puffy with sleep and he grimaced. But then he recognized me.

"My God, a famous person! You don't know me, do you? I went to a workshop you gave at the university. Kevin O'Connor."

We shook hands.

I didn't remember him. I apologized— I'd met a lot of people over the years— but he held the door open and waved me inside the apartment.

"Sorry to be so long answering, but I thought it was my father. He's always checking to see that I'm really writing."

The coffee table was littered with newspapers, potato-chip bags and library books. Unfolded laundry lay in an armchair and a vacuum cleaner stood in the middle of the room. The stereo and computer took up one wall. A chess game was on the computer screen.

"I'm supposed to be writing the great novel," he said and shrugged. "Don't tell me my father sent you. He wants me to sell shoes in his store!"

"Not a chance." Maybe his family had contributed the wreath, I thought, as I explained why I was here.

Suzanne Maloff! He laughed. Guys were always knocking at his door, looking for her. Clients. Lots of comings and goings. And a boyfriend fell asleep and burned a pizza in the oven, setting the smoke detector off! And before the firefighters arrived, the jerk yanked the alarm from the ceiling!

"I almost quit on the spot! The asshole! Man, it was a job getting everyone out and that punk just stood there looking shit-faced."

"You mean— you're the super?"

"Yeah. Eighty bucks off the rent. I live cheap."

He told me about his philosophy of life: take it easy and don't be a wage slave. He wrote two pages a day and he had enjoyed my workshop so much that he'd upped his quota to five, but the pressure got to him. The year before, he worked at Sears; now he was on unemployment insurance.

"So you have keys to all the apartments," I said after I had commiserated with him.

"What're you trying to say?"

We looked at each other.

"Jeez, I don't know. She could be in there fast asleep."

"She could be in there injured. Maybe she OD'd."

"I don't know."

"I just want to be sure she's all right. She definitely wanted to see me. About her son. You know what happened there?"

"The creep. She had him with her for a while here. He was stealing bicycles and selling them. The cops came. He was fixing them up in the parking lot!"

"Is that your Honda in the parking lot?"

"You mean my limo."

"Then it's the only car there. She must be out because her car's not there."

"You won't tell?"

"Of course not."

"I'll have to get a job if they fire me," he said, but he took a ring of keys out of the desk drawer. "Two minutes," he told me. "No, make that one minute.

"I can't believe I'm doing this," he added, as he inserted a key into Suzanne's shiny deadbolt. "She had a new lock put in after someone broke in."

Suzanne's letter had surprised me and her apartment surprised me more. One wall was papered in a red brick pattern and hung with brass plates. Plants were everywhere, hanging from the ceiling, on the wide windowsill and on top of a pine armoire that looked very much like mine. Red cushions dotted the black sofa, and there was a rocking chair draped with an afghan. A picture of a barn in a snowy field hung over the sofa and a braided rug covered the middle of the beige wall-to-wall carpeting.

The small kitchen was spotless, with a glass-topped table and more plants. A few steps brought me to the bedroom, where a quilt covered the brass bed and a big teddy bear wearing a red bow sat on a wooden chair. A black leather jacket, studded with silver, lay on the bed, and the top of the dresser was covered with make-up and perfume.

The telephone was shaped like a cat and the answering machine was next to it. The message light was flashing and I was tempted to press it, but Kevin would know and probably pass out. He was breathing hard by the front door.

Did I dare take the tape?

"What're you doing in there? Come on, let's get out of here."

"It's not what I expected," I said, back in his apartment.

Kevin flopped onto the couch.

"Atmosphere for the guys," he said. "I've never gone past her door."

"I liked her wallpaper," I said.

"Yeah."

"You ever talk to her?"

"Just to collect the rent. She doesn't speak to anyone in the building except to say hi, and sometimes she doesn't even do that. I think she thought someone here called the cops on her son, the little turkey. Creep. I guess he won't see daylight for a long time. I knew he was trouble the first time I laid eyes on him.

"His mother's trouble, too. I've seen her car at this motel on Highway 7. But some of them'll knock on her door, like I said. Or any door. Whichever one they like. They get mad when she's not in and just pound away."

"Well, you can always say you lived upstairs from a hooker, if that's what she is. I heard she did exotic dancing."

"Stripping. Guess what?" He didn't wait for me to answer. "Guess what was in her laundry? Lacy gloves! Suzanne forgot them on the machine. My girlfriend found them."

"The gloves must have been used in her act."

"Barb, that was my girlfriend's name, talked to her once. Green, I'm telling you. Barb told her that she must be proud of her son, looking after his bicycle so well!"

The dust in Kevin's apartment was getting to me. Even the vacuum cleaner was dusty.

"Does she ever have female guests?" I asked.

"Not that I ever saw. I really shouldn't have let you in there," Kevin said.

"We were checking to see if she was all right. One of her boyfriends could have beaten her up or worse. You're sure you haven't seen any women around her place?"

"Nope. I told you. No women."

He gave me an exasperated look. It was time to leave.

"I hate this job, you know," he said gloomily, and for the next fifteen minutes he recited sad tales about having to unlock doors in the middle of the night because a yahoo had locked himself out; about the guy on the third floor who hadn't paid his electricity bill and strung a cord to the apartment below. It was one hell of a life. But better than living in his parents' basement. Or working at a job.

Escape came when I mentioned Kevin's writing. No, he wasn't ready to have anyone read it. He wasn't even sure if he wanted to put himself through the suffering of sending it out...

I invited him to my writing class when I left. And I wished I had taken the tape.

Chapter Twenty-Three

I called Suzanne every two hours for the rest of the day, and each time left a message on her machine. Something was wrong, I thought, as I read Amanda's latest stories, which were about her two grandmothers and their female ancestors' imagined history. She had drawn maps and had had photos and postcards scanned.

The stories were wonderful, but I kept thinking about Suzanne. Where was she? What had happened? And what did she want to tell me?

I dreamt of Suzanne that night. Her long car was parked in a sunny field. Golden wheat waved in the summer breeze except for where Suzanne had driven. A grove of trees stood by the horizon.

The car doors were open. Music came from the radio— Willie Nelson— and Suzanne's feet, in red high heels, stretched out of the right door.

A voice said: "You really don't want to know, do you?"

I protested, but my feet wouldn't move and the voice cackled and sneered.

"I have glued your feet to the earth, you fool!"

Flies were buzzing around the car...

And then Neil was sitting in a western-style saloon. His gun lay on the bar.

"Is this the gun that framed you?" the bartender asked. "The gun that shot the woman?"

The dream haunted me as I drove to Toronto. The weather was like in the dream— warm and sunny, Indian summer, and the fields along the 401 glimmered. I would not have been surprised to see Suzanne's car there. And her red high heels sticking out.

I was glad to get to the city.

Mrs. Marguerite Dalby lived in a red brick house only blocks away from the Women's House. Correction: a dusty red brick house. A paper- and book-littered dusty red house. There was even a pile of weathered magazines on a wicker table on the wide verandah and a sticker on the window in the front door read, "Feed the..." Whoever or whatever was to be fed had worn off.

Mrs. Dalby was— bosomy. Smudged reading glasses, suspended by a black cord, dangled over her large front contained in a brown cardigan. Grey hair chopped short, a broad and smiling face. She shook my hand (while Robert beamed) and stuck the glasses on her upturned nose.

"Well, this is quite a kettle of fish, isn't it?" she said, holding my hand. "But I'm glad to meet you, Carolyn Archer."

"She's a fan," Robert said. "She's read all your books."

"And yours." She released my hand. "Surprising as they are. The clergy isn't what it used to be," she told me. "Nothing's the way it used to be, and a good thing, too. Come in, come in, I'm glad to meet you."

She ushered us into the cluttered front room. The window space was taken over by plants, including a very crooked cactus that stretched almost to the ceiling. It had nicked the curtain; the gauzy fabric was caught up beside an asparagus fern spilling over a tottery wicker stand. A half-finished sweater in a garish orange shade lay on top of a pile of papers on a brown chair, and a black cat was cleaning its paws on an arborite coffee table piled with library books. A huge bookcase spilled paperbacks, bright bestsellers, and faded tomes from the forties.

"Sit, sit." She picked a book off the brown settee draped with a green afghan. "I'll make tea, shall I? I've been on the phone all morning, trying to get through to the mayor's office, but they kept putting me on hold.

I'm sure it was one of those computer voices. They even have them at the library now."

"Now why would you be calling the mayor?" Robert asked, sinking back into the settee.

"For the local day care! There's money for everything except what matters most, it seems. But you can't tell a computer that!"

She bustled out. The cat gave me a wary look and jumped off the table. And what about Willy? I wondered, picking up the top library book. It was a biography of May Sarton, and beneath it was an old Ann Rule true-crime book.

"I wonder why she left the church," Robert mused. He had his hands folded nerdily in his lap. "She was such a great churchgoer."

Beneath the Rule book was an illustrated volume of cat stories. And beneath that, essays by prairie women.

Had Helena ever been here?

"Now here's the tea."

I moved the books so Mrs. Dalby could set the tray down. The teapot and cups looked like Royal Doulton. "I'm afraid I just have these little biscuits to offer you. I was planning to make muffins, but as I was saying, the phone kept me occupied.

"Not like the old days," she told Robert. "I remember my mother cleaning for days when the minister came calling! Shucks! I remember doing the same thing myself! Ridiculous, wasn't it? But women didn't know any better. I've made real tea. Can't stand the herbal stuff, but I keep it around for those who don't touch caffeine."

For a few minutes, she and Robert reminisced about the old Baptist church. This led to a discussion of Marguerite's disavowal of organized religion. She had always had an enquiring mind, she said, and been a great reader, but growing up in "old Toronto" had kept her toeing the line until she started attending protests. "I was a radical and I didn't know it," she said. "It's all about freedom and feeding the poor and looking after our planet."

"Still, church is a comfort for many," Robert said. He held the dainty teacup delicately on his knee.

"Comfort my foot! Why be comfortable when half the world is starving? And women are beaten and raped and children abused and animals decimated?"

But Marguerite Dalby seemed pretty comfortable to me.

"So you knew Helena," I said.

"I did. She sat on the very spot where you are sitting now. I lent her books and she returned them."

"What kind of books? What did she like to read?" I thought of the sentimental verses in the album.

"Actually, I lent her literary magazines. I had some old copies of *The Fiddlehead* and others. And *Canadian Forum*— I've been a subscriber for years. She said she liked to write poetry, you see, and I must say I don't like modern verse, no rules, it seems— why, I remember writing sonnets in high school. But the mags wouldn't hurt, I thought, and brought them along to the centre."

"The Women's House," I said.

"That's right. I left them for her. She wasn't there for the Kitchen Table Talks every week. That's what they're called: Kitchen Table Talks. Women gathering around, talking about whatever's on their minds. Current issues, political things, but sometimes it's just an old-fashioned gabfest."

"Did Helena contribute much?"

"Well, now, I don't know what to say about that... She'd sit there quietly and you'd forget all about her being there but if she disagreed she'd say it loud and clear. There was something about her... I don't know. She wasn't unpleasant, and we encourage women to express themselves, we want them to be honest, but she had a way of, how shall I say it? She had a way of not exactly putting people off, but of making them uncomfortable. She had a rather direct way of talking."

"Sounds bossy," Robert said.

"No, not bossy. More resentful. I always had the feeling that she didn't really like us. She'd say, 'Look, I don't agree with this at all.' And that was fine. But you could feel the anger. I'll give you an example. We were discussing showing a film about wife abuse and she wanted us to invite the local MP and pretty well order him to come. If he didn't come, we should go to the media, she said. We should picket his house if he didn't turn up, she said.

"It was the way she said it, daring us not to agree. She'd stare us down. Later, we found out about her rape, and that seemed to explain things a bit... It was an awful thing that happened, of course; just another example of patriarchy and male power and I've seen it all my life, in the church, too."

"Things are changing," Robert said, but Marguerite disagreed and they spent a few minutes sparring.

"How did you find out about the rape?" I asked when there was a lull in the conversation.

"She told us at a talk. She made an announcement. She was very upfront about it, and everyone was immediately comforting, saying how brave she was, and what was she going to do about it? She'd been seeing a therapist, she said."

"Was the therapist's name Tatiana, by any chance?" I asked.

"Tatiana? That's interesting. Helena would never tell us whom she was seeing. It was always 'my therapist.' My therapist says this, my therapist says that."

"When I met her father, he spoke angrily about a Tatiana. He seemed to think Tatiana was someone at the Women's House."

"I can't recall anyone by that name. Women do come and go. Someone will drop in and never return, but I can't remember a Tatiana. Robert tells me you know the policeman who raped Helena."

And before I could answer her, she went to make more tea.

"It seemed best to be honest," Robert confessed. He set his empty cup on the table. The cat jumped up and sniffed.

"Shouldn't I have told her?" Robert snatched his cup away from the cat.

But Marguerite was back.

"Have to wait for the water to boil. Kettle takes forever. I hope you're not dying of thirst. Here."

She put a copy of *Prairie Fire* on the table. It was an issue devoted to Anne Szumigalski.

"As I said, I'm not much of a one for modern poetry, but I specifically remembered this *Prairie Fire* because they wrote about Szumigalski living in a veteran's house and way back when, when I was first married, we lived in a veteran's house. See my name inside?"

She opened it and there was her name, written on the first page.

"This was one of the magazines I lent Helena. When I asked if she'd enjoyed it, she became angry and said I'd never given it to her. That's what I mean about Helena being confrontational. I didn't argue or disagree with her. It's only a magazine and perhaps she'd lost it or maybe it had fallen out of her bag on her way home.

"A few days later, who should appear at my door, but Helena. She had the other magazines with her to 'prove' that I hadn't given her this one. 'I don't steal,' she said. 'Of course you don't,' I said and I made tea. But she wouldn't let it drop. She said, 'I just didn't want you to get the wrong impression. I just wanted to clear things.' I agreed with everything she said and we had a nice visit after that."

"Was this after she talked about the rape?" I asked. "After seeing the therapist?"

"No. It was before. But here is the strange thing. She had this big green bag and she'd leave it open. I could see my *Prairie Fire* inside. She guarded that bag with her life— it was crammed with notebooks and medicine and whatnot— but I saw my chance when she felt sick one day and rushed to the bathroom. I reached in and took it and saw it was mine."

"What did you do?"

Marguerite smiled. "Helena wasn't the only one with a roomy purse."

"What did she do?"

"There's my kettle. You'll get more tea yet."

She bustled out of the room.

"Tricky Helena," I said to Robert. "It looks better for Neil."

"But stealing a book isn't a defense," Robert said.

"Dishonesty might be. I've heard about other tall tales. She said she visited her relatives in the States, but she never did."

Marguerite returned with the teapot.

"We'll just let it steep. But to answer your question: Helena couldn't very well do anything, could she? She was sick to her stomach, had eaten something, but she noticed the book was gone at once. She gave me a look... It wasn't a nice look. She knew that I knew she'd lied and I knew she knew, but there was nothing said. She didn't do anything, but she'd give me this look, like she was waiting to get even."

"And then she told about the rape," I said.

"Yes, but she never forgot what I'd discovered. She still gave me the same look. She held her grudges."

"Did you tell anyone about the magazine thing?"

"No, it seemed petty. Someone might have confronted her and then it would have been my word against hers. I wasn't getting into a silly battle like that. And women who steal often have suffered sexual abuse."

"She dared you to confront her," I said.

"She was toying with me," Marguerite said.

"Do you believe she was raped?" I asked.

"I don't know. I just don't know."

"Neil's a nice man," I said. "I don't believe he sexually assaulted her."

Marguerite sighed. "I like to give people the benefit of the doubt."

"So do I," I said.

"His revolver killed her. No one deserves that," Marguerite said.

"I think someone else shot her. And Neil wouldn't have left his revolver lying around after he shot her! The real killer left the gun to frame Neil."

"Unless he panicked," Marguerite said. "He could have heard someone coming and panicked."

"Not Neil. Neil's used to guns."

"Why would someone want to frame him?" Marguerite asked.

"He's worked as an undercover cop. He made all kinds of enemies."

Marguerite nodded, but she looked sceptical. She returned to the subject of Helena.

"She was a complicated woman, and she made her own complications, but they were petty ones. They wouldn't be a motive for murder. And murdering her to frame this police officer..."

She poured the tea.

"I wonder if the women at the House urged her to press charges," Robert mused. "What if she made up this story and the only way to validate it was to do what the women said?"

"'What the women said!' Really, Robert. We're not in the army at the Women's House!"

"It is a thought, however," Robert persisted.

"Huh! And if she had accused him unjustly, might that not be a motive for murder? The man's reputation and career ruined, his life a waste? Think about it. And the same thing holds true if she didn't fabricate a story in the first place.

"It was his gun that killed her," Marguerite finished quietly. "He could have panicked and dropped it."

Robert shook his head. His teacup wobbled as he set it down. Marguerite took it from him. Her wedding china, she chuckled. Darn stuff.

"I liked the memorial service," I said. "Did you meet Helena's mother?"

She hadn't. But— "Helena used to talk about her rich relatives in the States."

"Her father was a draft dodger."

"He came from money, Helena said. His family wanted her to come and live with them in their big house with the winding staircase and the swimming pool out back."

"I don't think she ever visited them."

"She spoke about them taking her to New York City, to the Empire State Building. She said her father wouldn't go back to New York for a million dollars. He liked nature and the outdoors. A homebody, she called him."

"He married a local woman and stayed on in this little hamlet way north of Toronto. He's a vegetarian who makes trouble for hunters. You can imagine how that goes over up there."

"Oh, yes. I have relatives in the Great Canadian North. Poor Helena."

"You would think if her father came from a well-to-do family, he would have wanted more for his kids," I said. "I met him briefly. He didn't strike me as a contented person, even given the fact that I saw him right after Helena's funeral. I don't think he has many friends. I wondered when I met him what he was doing in that backwater."

"Not everyone needs glitz and glamour," Robert said.

"You say 'not many friends,' but I believe the family was close," Marguerite said.

"He hated the Women's House," I said. "You probably heard that he didn't want his wife to go to the memorial service. I think the hate was all tied up with this Tatiana person no one seems to know."

"People do and say surprising things when they grieve," Marguerite said.

This got Robert going on funerals he had conducted. Marguerite added stories from the old days and said she preferred the more personalized memorial services today to the "Hail, Fire and Brimstone" funerals she remembered. This led to a discussion of familiar ritual.

I picked up *Prairie Fire* and flipped through it. In the back was a subscription coupon. Someone had drawn hearts all over it, but Helena had filled in her name and address.

Helena had lived at 235 Clayburn.

The street where Maureen had followed Jane.

An old woman wearing a black babushka was sweeping the sidewalk in front of 235 Clayburn.

She spat when I introduced myself as "Helena's cousin from the States."

"You go! I call police! You tell lies. The other one tell lies, too!"

Two-thirty-five Clayburn was a tall, narrow brick house in a row of houses squished side by side; barely a yard separated each place from its neighbour. There were two mailboxes by the front door.

"I'm sorry. The other one? I don't understand..."

"I'm a clergyman," Robert said. "Perhaps I can help."

She waved her broom at us.

"You go! I call police!"

"Did you let someone in?" I asked.

She shook her broom, but I could tell from her face that I had guessed right.

Chapter Twenty-Four

Something was wrong. There was something I was missing. Helena Quintham was turning out to be a far more complicated woman than the sad creature I had imagined. A storyteller, a person who wove riddles for their own sake and liked to keep people guessing. An enigma: she didn't fit in, had never fit in, yet she seemed to have had this inner confidence, a haughtiness that perhaps had come from her father. Growing up in Beaver Falls, she was the different girl, the girl who didn't have jeans and sneakers like the others. And her father wasn't like other fathers.

Had Wilbur convinced her of her otherness? *You are special, Helena. Forget the local rednecks. You don't want to be like everyone else.*

But if he had convinced her of her superiority, he hadn't encouraged education, formal or otherwise. I thought of the sentimental verses in the album. Why hadn't he shared books with her, or even the sixties' songs he must have played on his guitar?

Had he given up his ideals? No, he still had strong views on not killing animals...

Did Helena think her father had let her down? The boys in the family had gone to college.

Or did she model herself more on her mother, an ordinary country-woman?

But that didn't feel right, either.

Wilbur... if only I had tried a different approach when I met him. Who was he? What was his story?

An idealistic draft dodger. A kid. He comes to Canada in his van, finds a spot under the trees in Beaver Falls and plays his guitar. Pot smoker, long-haired hippie. People shake their heads...

He takes up with Helena's mother. No, he meets her in a restaurant; they talk. He says, "Drop on by some time," and she does. She's a gawky teenager, a small-town girl, he's never met anyone quite as naive or innocent. She's the real McCoy: how much closer to the land can you get?

Drifting off to sleep, I could see Mary: chunky in jeans, wearing a cheap pink top as she giggled, sitting on the steps of the van... the open back door. Smoking up for the first time: she's heard of dope, of course, but to smoke it! This is really something! She feels as sophisticated as the girls in New York! Hey— she's a doper now! She's crossed some line, and she thinks— when she's going to school (grade eleven, twelve?), or teaching Sunday school— she thinks: if they only knew!

Soon she's out at the van all the time. She... oh, she can't be so small-town, sure she'll sunbathe nude, she'll pretend she knows the songs he plays on his guitar.

And he... he's enthralled by her country tales. He's never known anyone who burned wood before, or whose mother baked bread or whose father planted a big vegetable garden. These country ways are so real, more natural than the Long Island suburbia he comes from, the patios and barbecues and three cars in the garage...

Will she live with him? Hey, it'll be cool.

But that's a line she's not sure she can cross. When her girlfriends fall in love, they get engaged and have showers.

Besides, her father has been making scenes about her trips to the van. Folks are talking. She's always been a good girl; what's wrong with her?

She becomes pregnant... Wilbur panics. In a day he can be in Quebec, in four days he can be in British Columbia. He never meant to stay here, not in Beaver Falls. No way!

He wants to go home... He even wants to see his awful, materialistic family. But then he'll be arrested...

Mary is weepy and saying she wants to die and her father comes out to the van and threats and curses fill the air... words that everyone will later pretend were never said. And Wilbur claims he loves Helena and to hell with everyone else.

So... marriage, a baby, a house. More kids. The years pass and his wife never smokes pot again and doesn't pretend any more that she likes his songs. She has more important business: raising her kids.

He digs in. He does love his kids and a life is created, an existence... He never forgets that this life is not one he would ever have chosen if it hadn't been for escaping the draft. He's a stubborn man: he makes the best of things, but he keeps to himself. He can be testy and his wife manages as well as she can...

He has always thought that when the kids were grown, he would take off.

But where? To what?

I was almost asleep, but I could picture his family back home: the father would drive a Cadillac, the mother would have dyed red hair, done weekly. Business people...

And Helena: different, sly, inventing complications, holding grudges.

A woman like Helena would have enemies.

But why *Jane*? She could have killed Helena without using Neil's gun.

That was the key: Neil's gun. And who had used it.

This time, I dreamt of Helena's house. Mary Quintham waved from the window and Wilbur... Wilbur was in the woods, playing his guitar. He was smiling and suntanned and then he was leaning over a woman... I could see her, but Helena was saying, "I always roll my pie crust out on wax paper." She was in a kitchen, the kitchen I had imagined, and even in the dream I knew the room was a fantasy.

Tatiana sat on a kitchen chair, watching.

She kept her back to me.

The dream reminded me of the one about Suzanne.

By eleven, I was at Kevin O'Connor's place. Surely he would be up? His little Honda was in the parking lot. I pounded and pounded on his door and I was about to leave when he appeared. He wore blue striped pyjamas. And slippers.

"Writing all night," he mumbled, as if he had to explain why he slept so late.

"I was just driving by and I noticed your car in the lot," I said.

"Didn't get to bed until four... Jeez." He shook his head and squeezed his eyes shut. Behind him, his place looked murky.

"She was back," he whispered. He looked in the direction of Suzanne's door. "Her car was there and I heard her in the apartment but she wasn't there long. Last I saw was her car heading out."

"Maybe I should leave her a note." I had a notebook in my purse, but the bag was in the car. "You wouldn't have a piece of paper, would you?"

He wasn't happy to let me in. The drapes were drawn and a pizza box and two empty beer bottles sat next to discarded socks on the floor. He had to turn a light on to find computer paper.

"Writing can be a real bitch," he said, as he handed me the paper. "No one knows how hard you have to work."

"I used to write a lot at night, too. You wouldn't happen to have a pen, would you?"

"Yeah, sure." But he had to rummage. Two were out of ink and the third one turned out to be a highlighter. Finally he found a working Bic in the kitchen.

I wrote: *I'm sorry we missed each other at the mall. Please call me. I would like to talk to you.*

"When was Suzanne back?"

"Couple of nights ago. I just made out the taillights of her car."

"It's funny she went off again so soon."

Kevin shrugged.

"Well, I'll just tuck this under her door. Too bad you didn't speak to her."

"What for? Why?"

"You could have made up an excuse. You could have said I was looking for her. Has anyone else been here?"

"Not that I know of."

I folded the paper.

"Is that normal? I thought guys were at her door all the time."

"Not lately..."

"I just wonder if she's okay. Maybe we could check..."

That brought him to life.

"No way! Not again! She could come back and catch us! Are you crazy?"

He watched while I slid my note under Suzanne's door. "How could she be in there if she's gone away?" he whispered.

He was right.

"You'll call me if you hear anything? If she comes back?"

"Yeah, sure. Sure."

Somehow I doubted if he would.

I had an uneasy feeling.

Chapter Twenty-Five

But Kevin did call. I recognized his nervous voice right away. At eight-thirty in the morning!

"Carolyn? Is this Carolyn Archer?"

"It's me, Kevin. Or rather, it is I. What gives? Why are you up so early?"

"I haven't even been to bed. I was writing..." His voice trailed off. "I mean... someone was around looking for you. Burton's lawyer, this lady lawyer."

"What?"

"Yesterday. Like, it was late afternoon and I just came back from the plaza and she was waiting for me. She wanted to know if I'd seen, you know, Suzanne, and I said about her coming back and all that, and she asked was I sure, because no one's heard from her and she wasn't in to visit Burton all week. She's in every other day to see him, and she hasn't been there. At the correctional centre, I mean.

"One of these real lawyer types, in a suit, you know? Kind of woman my mother's always trying to introduce me to. The type who wants a monster home and three cars. It was like she had me on the witness stand! Honestly! She kept saying, 'Are you sure she was back here? Did you see her? How do you know it was her if you didn't actually see her?' and then she asked to use my phone and I thought of saying it was out of order, but she barged right in and made her call and then she started again.

"'Has anyone been around looking for her?' she asked next and..."

"You told her I was," I finished for him.

"Yeah. I wish I hadn't said. She's going to call you, she says, and I thought before she called you I'd better warn you."

"I won't say you let me into Suzanne's apartment," I said. "Of course I won't say anything! Don't worry!"

"I said you came looking for Suzanne 'cause she didn't turn up for a meeting."

"That's fine."

"Not a word about the apartment."

"Of course not."

He rambled on for a while about what would happen if "they" found out he had let someone into a tenant's apartment.

"Look, Kevin, I've already forgotten about it. My lips are sealed. Believe me. What's this lawyer's name?"

Gillian O'Rourke, he told me.

"Something fishy is going on," he said. "Something is definitely rotten in the state of Denmark."

The phone rang again at precisely nine o'clock. Gillian O'Rourke wanted to see me as soon as possible. We settled on eleven, at her office in a strip mall on the outskirts of Guelph.

Kevin O'Connor would never be a writer. His powers of observation were too slack. Gillian O'Rourke was not the slim sleek suit of the future monster home, but a chunky woman whose navy suit— at least he'd gotten that right— was cheap and too tight. Her nails were bitten, she wore no make-up, and her short hair needed a trim. But her grin was appealing and I liked the off-hand, friendly way she waved me to a seat— a seat covered with newspapers and files.

I moved the pile to the floor.

"What a mess. I need a Boy Friday. Sorry. So. So! You and I have both been looking for Suzanne Maloff. Burton's mother."

Gillian listened while I explained about the appointment Suzanne had missed, and shook her head when I related the phone threats and the fist fight in the street.

"She is not exactly Miss America, is she? I've had my own run-ins with her, right in this office. No hair pulling, however, I am glad to say. She wanted me to get bail for Burton, but that was a no-go. She seems to feel I'm in cahoots with the cops or some such thing."

"She says Burton didn't kill his grandmother. She had information for me, she said. Something important to tell me. She even wrote me a letter, so it must have mattered a great deal to her."

Should I mention Neil?

"And then she didn't show," Gillian said.

"That's right."

"No one has seen or heard from her for a week. She visits Burton every chance she has, and I don't think there's been a day when she hasn't phoned me. Until she went missing."

"You think she's missing?"

"What else can I think? It's mighty strange, wouldn't you say? She'd hardly take a holiday with her kid in the slammer. She might be a pretty tough cookie, but she's there for Burton no matter what."

"She'd naturally think he didn't do it."

"Yes, she would. But I'm inclined to think she's correct. I don't think Burton killed his grandmother, either. It's true he hasn't been a bundle of joy, but I think he's telling the truth when he says he didn't murder his grandmother."

"The police were there the week before, I heard."

"Maria didn't call them. A neighbour did. A neighbour who heard some yelling. It's true they argued. Burton wanted money to buy a new motorcycle and Grandma said no. Not that I blame her. I wouldn't give anyone money for a new motorcycle, either.

"But the real trouble between Burton and his grandmother was over his mother. Maria would say things about Suzanne and Burton would fly off the handle."

"I didn't know Maria. I saw her sometimes when I visited her neighbour. She was often working in the garden."

"An old-world woman. She didn't mince words, apparently. She'd never heard about child psychology, about the inadvisability of bad-mouthing a child's parent."

"Maybe she bad-mouthed Suzanne and he hit her."

"But Burton didn't see his grandmother that day! He hit her *another* day. As I said, 'not a bundle of joy.' He says he didn't shoot her and that an undercover cop was on the street that day."

"That's a new one."

"That's what Suzanne wanted to tell you, that someone else was hanging around. Burton thought it was about drugs. He isn't lily-white by any means. So he kept going."

I shook my head.

"You never know," Gillian said. "An undercover woman cop, he said. But the woman could have been someone else entirely."

"So where was this woman cop?"

"Parked down the street. Always in another car, he said. Burton notices vehicles."

"So... Burton thinks this so-called undercover cop killed his grandmother???" I shook my head. "That's pretty far out, I'd say."

"That's one theory. He owes someone money and they might try to get back at Burton..."

"You don't even sound convincing to me."

"I know. But what else is there?"

"The police must have other evidence."

"They do. The usual things: fingerprints and so on. But he was in and out of his grandmother's house a lot. I can't really discuss the evidence more specifically with you."

"Why would Suzanne want to tell me about this... undercover policewoman, or Mafia hit woman, or whatever this person was? Why me?"

"Because she felt I didn't believe her. You're right. It does sound far-fetched."

"But then she disappeared."

"Then she disappeared."

"So now what?"

"I don't know. I really don't. Burton seems to think his mother had more information."

"So we have to find his mother. The superintendent in her building says Suzanne came back."

"But he didn't see her, did he? Do you know him?"

"Kevin? He was at a workshop I gave, but I didn't remember him."

"Quite the oddball. I think I scared the hell out of him. He looked pretty guilty about something."

"He's worried about his father sending a spy to report on him," I said brightly, hoping Gillian would not know I was lying. She was sharp, though, and I changed the subject. "How often did Burton see this other so-called spy?"

"On his grandmother's street? Just three times, but he claims someone was following him around."

"Paranoia, especially if he's involved with drugs."

"But the question is, what did Suzanne want to tell you?" Gillian looked at me. "Maybe Suzanne found out who this person was."

"Maybe."

"If she doesn't surface within twenty-four hours I'm going to report her missing," Gillian said.

I thought of the dream I had had about Suzanne.

Chapter Twenty-Six

No, Bron told me on the phone, she had not noticed anyone suspicious parked on the street. There had been some pesky magazine salespeople, but they were young men who offered free paper towels if she signed up for their offer. They had come back twice, forgetting they had called earlier. But she had no idea if they had a vehicle or not.

But she did have news. Maureen had followed Jane to— a fertility clinic!

"So that could be a motive! She could be blaming Neil for her infertility problems."

"What does Neil say about that?"

"Neil doesn't know what Maureen's doing. He has no idea."

"I hope Jane doesn't recognize Maureen."

"Not a chance. I wouldn't know her myself in her boy's clothes."

"You sound better, Bron."

"Things don't look as dark. And Maureen and I seem to be getting along okay these days, although Mr. Asshole still drives me crazy. I didn't get the job, by the way. I guess I didn't suit the old dame who interviewed me. So that's another grievance Bruce has. Do you think people would think it was awful of me if I came on the retreat?"

"Of course not.Too bad about the job, Bron."

"Yeah, well. I couldn't have gone on the retreat if I'd been hired. Maureen wants me to go and Neil thinks I should go, too. It's still set for next weekend?"

"It sure is. It'll be good to see you again."

"It'll be great to see *you* again. And guess what? I've been writing in my notebook. Writing like crazy, stories about young married life and love."

"I can hardly wait to read what you've done. Should I pick you up on the way?"

"I am taking the bus! Bruce wants to drive me— not only to be sure

I get away so he can have his privacy for the weekend, the bugger, but because he's heard rumours that the lodge where the you're having the retreat might be for sale, or will be soon, and he and his big lawyer buddies have been looking for an investment. But no way am I driving in a car with Bruce. I told him I'd take the bus— another adventure for me. So I guess I'll take the bus! He can look his investment over another time and not be so sneaky about it!"

I knew I had to tell Peter about Bruce and his friends being interested in the lodge.

"Well, doesn't that take the cake!" Peter said when I told him. "How on earth did they find out? You didn't tell anyone that the lodge was for sale, did you?"

"I think I mentioned it to Neil when he called..."

"Neil???"

"But he didn't tell Bron. She knew nothing about it."

"Why did you tell Neil?"

"I guess it just slipped out. It wasn't a secret or anything. I didn't think it was, Peter. And who was Neil going to tell?"

"His lawyer."

"Anyway, I don't know why you're so worried. Bill and Linda said we'd have the first chance. They won't sell to anyone else if we're interested."

"What if someone comes up with cold, hard cash? How can they turn that down?"

"Because they gave their word, that's why."

"But we haven't made an offer. Not officially."

"So you want to make a definite offer?"

"Don't you?"

"I think so."

"Think so?"

"I don't... Peter, if you really and truly want to buy the lodge and live in Meredith, if you want it so much, I'll go along with it."

"But you're not sure?"

"I don't know about living in Meredith," I said. "I'm not sure how I feel about that. I guess I'm worried about being in such a small place."

"That's it, then," Peter said. "We'll forget about it."

"No, we won't forget about it. Can't we wait and see? Linda and Bill said we'd have first chance. If Bruce and his lawyer buddies make an offer, we can still decide."

"And here I thought you were for it!"

"I am for it. I mean... I'm not against it. I just want to give this more thought."

"And what if we have to make our minds up, all at once?"

"Then we'll go for it. And if it doesn't work out, we can always sell the place again."

"And what if we can't sell it? What then?"

"Let's wait and see," I said.

"You didn't call the realtor in Maine, did you?" Peter asked.

"Not yet," I confessed.

He didn't say anything.

"But the retreat is coming up. I need to do some real thinking, Peter. A retreat is just the place to think."

"I don't want the lodge if you're not a hundred per cent in favour," Peter said. "And if you're not for it..."

"What then?"

"We'll just go on the way we are," Peter said.

Chapter Twenty-Seven

Suzanne was still missing by the time I drove to Meredith— alone. I'd considered offering Amanda a ride, but I needed time for myself.

The hardest thing about buying the lodge, I realized, was that I would have to sell my grandmother's property in Maine. Yes, I would phone Nicholas Pierce, the realtor who looked after the rental for me— as soon as the retreat was over. For sure, I promised Peter. Just to enquire...

But I couldn't imagine actually selling my old childhood home. It was true that I hadn't been back in years.

I was sure Peter remembered the last time I was there. I had gone to Maine by myself after my friend Millicent died. The house was between tenants and I needed to be alone. I slept in my old bedroom and stayed up all night drinking tea and re-reading my childhood books. I walked on the beach and rode my old bicycle to the village. It was a solitary but not lonely time and when Peter came on a foggy day in August, I was imagining myself staying forever, growing older in the big wooden house and becoming one of those eccentric women who joined the historical society, spied on birds and made rosehip jam.

I was so used to the idea of the house being there. It was something to return to, the possibility of another life, or a break from the life I did have. A return to the person I'd been long before Peter or Guelph.

And on Monday (or Tuesday or... Friday) I'd pick up the telephone and ask my old school friend about putting the house on the market.

In Meredith, I dropped in to see Marion and Hugh, who were not, to my surprise, overjoyed about the possibility of us buying the lodge. Marion was adamant that she didn't want to give up the B & B, "and Peter doesn't know what he's talking about. Two women in one household! We'd be at each other's throats in no time."

"Peter gets these ideas," Hugh said. "What does he know about hotel keeping? And that big mortgage! You could lose everything."

"I'm sorry Hugh's worrying," I told Marion in the kitchen. "He doesn't need any worries now."

Marion was silent as she poured the tea.

"Peter's so tired of the bookstore," I went on. "I had no idea he felt that way. It's getting older, feeling he hasn't accomplished very much."

"He was never very happy in Meredith," Marion said. "It's a big step to leave the life you've built in Guelph." She passed me a cup of tea. "And I must say I'll miss having a place to go to in civilization."

"There's always Allison," I said.

Marion didn't respond to that.

"And when I get fed up with the woods you and I can take off for Toronto," I said.

"You're already plotting your escape," Marion said, as the phone rang.

It was Bron, waiting to be picked up at the bus station, which was at Miller's Hardware.

"How is Neil doing?" Marion asked, after I hung up. "I still find it unbelievable. Such a nice man."

"It's unbelievable, all right. I know he's innocent. But things are looking up. His lawyer has a private investigator hired and... there've been some developments."

Had Peter confided in Marion about Neil and me? I wondered. Midnight chats while he was here consoling her?

"I've found out quite a bit more about the woman who was killed." I had told her— briefly— about what I'd learned in Beaver Falls. "I'll fill you in later. Don't forget dinner tomorrow night with the budding writers." I had invited Marion for dinner at the lodge on Saturday. "I'd better collect Bron."

Frances Harley was complaining to Amanda about her room when Bron and I arrived at the lodge.

"It is right over the lounge! I'll never sleep, and the curtains let in too much light!" Her hands were clenched and I was amused to see that she was wearing slacks— ugly beige polyester pants, but slacks all the time. Usually our Frances wore expensive wool skirts.

"Maybe they can change your room," I suggested to Frances.

"It's the last single. I can't share with anyone."

"All that good fresh air will knock you out in no time," Bron said. "Fresh air and writing will put you right to sleep. What a wonderful place!" she exclaimed to me, looking around the bright front room with the pine chairs and red curtains. "Put me in a cell and I won't complain!"

Amanda winked at me. She wore a long denim skirt and a sheepskin vest and looked great, as did Bron, who had jeans on and an over-sized white shirt. Maureen's influence, perhaps.

Frances grumbled that perhaps she had better drive home.

"It really is wonderful," Amanda said as we strolled to the lake while Bron was settling into her room and Frances was waiting to see Linda about her complaints. "All this serenity and the lake and the fall air, the gorgeous red leaves. I'm not going to want to leave when the weekend is over."

The woods smelled of pine, and down by the lake, wood smoke came from one of the log cabins. The water lapped against the rocks and suddenly a loon lifted into the air.

"Let's walk down to the lake," I said.

"Canoes," Amanda said. "I haven't been in a canoe in ages. Do you think we can take them out?"

"I don't see why not."

"And look, the cabins have porches. You could sit and watch the lake at dusk. Oh, smell the wood smoke. Too bad we couldn't have stayed in the cabins."

"They've got hunters up from the States."

"A cabin would be a wonderful place to write, though, wouldn't it? You'd think you were at the centre of the universe, with nothing to distract you."

"You're a witch," I said, and Amanda looked at me quizzically. "I have something to tell you."

Why not tell her about Peter wanting to buy the lodge?

Everyone loved the place. By the time we sat down to eat Friday night, even Frances was cheerful. Linda had arranged a single table for us— "the round table"— and as we lifted our wine glasses for a toast to "Writers of the World" I almost felt that I could live here.

Especially if writers came to visit, I thought as I looked around the table at the students who had become so familiar. Marsha and friend, Betsy, both wearing new flannel shirts which they must have bought together, couldn't stop smiling. I had never seen Frederick so relaxed and imagined him, a Gregory Peck look-alike, whittling away on a piece of wood. Brad and Charlene seemed more down-to-earth in faded jeans. And Bella, Greg: her reddish mop of hair leaned forward as she whispered in Greg's young ear. Frances had changed back into a skirt— maybe that was why she was happier, I thought as she chatted with Amanda and Roberta. Whose ugly blue plastic earrings matched the blue dolphins in her sweater. But tonight I loved these earrings.

Observing my friends in the glow of the candlelight, I felt moved. We had come together because of our love of writing— and... here we were, together. Whatever troubles were out there, we were temporarily away from them. On retreat from the world.

"Look at this place," Marsha said. "It's fantastic! I'd move up here in a minute." Her cheeks glowed above her red shirt.

"I'll join you," Betsy said, and Charlene, Brad's wife, said the lodge reminded her of summers in Muskoka ("the same piney smell!"). Bella said, "Forget Europe. I know where I'm coming on my holidays next year," while Amanda gave me a secret smile. Roberta said she already felt "the creative juices flowing" and Frederick struck up a conversation with the American hunters. "The world comes to your door in a place like this." Our budding Sci-Fi writer wondered about renting a cabin and Brad said it was good to get away from the rat race. Once he made his money writing, he was going to look for a northern place.

Only Bron was quiet— a bit downcast. Because she was the only one not drinking wine? I caught her glancing at the wine bottle, and when Brad ordered another, she fiddled with her glass, and when I looked again, the glass had disappeared from the table.

But she cheered up down by the lake. Linda and Bill had laid on a fire in the largest cabin, and we spent the evening reading stories and drinking cocoa. Bron's story about shoplifting from the dime store when she was ten met with applause, and when she went outside to have a smoke, there were more comments about her work: the hiatus had done her good, and wasn't it something that she could write "with the pressure she's been under?"

I was looking forward to reading the stories Bron had written in Toronto and which she had given me earlier, but as usual it was Amanda's story I liked the best.

She wrote wittily and naughtily about her summer selling cosmetics at Eaton's in Toronto. She had to practise with her own make-up, creating "hills and hollows" from a book of diagrams given to her by her supervisor, Cynthia, who said, "Think of your face as an empty canvas. You have to work to make yourself beautiful. You can turn your face into a work of art."

The fiction was Cynthia's imagined life: making herself beautiful in her beige apartment at the end of the streetcar line.

"I think I want to send your stories to my publisher," I told Amanda, later, over a nightcap at the bar.

"You'd really do that?" She opened her eyes wide.

"Sure thing. No promises, though. Jake isn't too hot on short-story collections any more. A couple bombed and sold only a few hundred copies. But yours are wonderful. And if he doesn't take them, maybe he'll have a creative idea or two. And your stories aren't really fiction in the traditional sense..."

I was interrupted by Linda, who slid into a chair at our table.

"Everything all right? All the customers happy?"

I said: "Everything is wonderful!"

And it was. After an early breakfast buffet, my writers spanned out over the lodge. It was warm for October and Roberta and Bella settled on the porch of the cabin we had used the night before. Brad elected to write in his room, while Charlene went for a drive to Meredith, and Marsha and Betsy wrote in the lounge. Bron, "all written out," read in the garden and the others dispersed who-knew-where.

I started out writing in the lodge, drifted to the "shoppe," where I bought the new *Canadian Forum* and *Books in Canada*, and started reading Bron's stories in the empty dining room, but the outdoors was so lovely that I went for a walk to the lake, stopping only to wave at Bella and Roberta who were scribbling away.

I didn't write. But I wasn't disappointed, because I thought that the day would come when I would write in a cabin, and as I walked along the path by the lake, I pictured the big chair by the window, the bookcase, the red kettle for tea-making...

But I couldn't think about selling my grandmother's house, I realized, as I sat down in the dining room to read Bron's stories about her early days with Neil.

Linda had arranged box lunches and I took mine to the lake, where Bron was sitting on the dock and smoking. Amanda joined us briefly, but she was "really on a roll" and took her notebook and her lunch farther along the shore.

"Your writing is really coming along," I told Bron. I had retrieved her stories from the dining room, where I had left them, and finished another two before lunch.

She had written insightfully about being alone with Maureen until the weekends, when she and Neil socialized with cops and their wives. I liked the details about houses: the red kitchen tiles; the whatnot with its figurines of kittens and girls watering flowers; the wedding photo on a doily.

"The stories have helped me put things into perspective," she said. "Whatever happens now, however Neil's situation turns out, I realize I'm my own person..."

We were still talking when Bill came down to the lake and told me I had a long-distance phone call.

A frantic, panicky Kevin O'Connor told me that Suzanne's body had been discovered in her car in an abandoned barn north of Guelph.

Peter had told him where I was.

Chapter Twenty-Eight

"What? Slow down, Kevin!" I made my voice commanding, but I knew I had been expecting something like this. I saw my dream and Suzanne's feet in their red shoes...

"They're searching her apartment! They've got police ribbons out and what should I do? What if they find your fingerprints?"

I didn't hesitate.

"You'll have to tell them the truth, Kevin."

He couldn't! No way! There was no way he was jeopardizing his future!

What if he went to jail?

What if they suspected *him*?

"Don't be silly, Kevin. Now, tell me what happened."

"I don't know! They just said they found her body in this old barn! I don't know anything else! They woke me up and told me and I was writing all night and just got up! Two cops came and should I call that lawyer?"

On and on he went, and half an hour went by before I convinced him he had to tell the police I was in Suzanne's apartment— they'd find the fingerprints anyway— before he hung up.

After that, there was no more writing. Or reading.

I went to find Bron to tell her but she wasn't at the lake. Bella called out that Bron had gone for a walk around the lake, and I set out along the path, which at least gave me something to do because my heart was pounding.

And it was a good thing I went because halfway around the lake, I discovered Charlene, unconscious, with a big gash to the side of her head. Her eyes were closed and her legs splayed over a fallen log. There was blood all over her pink sweater. Her fuzzy pink sweater, the faded jeans, moccasin shoes with tassels. Her speckled grey socks, country socks. The orange autumn leaves, the fall grass... It was an unreal tableau.

I screamed.

"Well, at least no one can get Neil for this one," Bron said. "And I sure as hell didn't do it, because I never saw her."

It was nine o'clock. The ambulance had rushed Charlene to the Meredith Hospital and she had been airlifted, with Brad, to Sunnybrook in Toronto, because of head injuries. She hadn't regained consciousness.

The police had been here in the person of Guy Boudreau, Meredith's new Chief of Police, followed shortly by the OPP, who had questioned all of us and taken our names and addresses. They had even talked to the hunters.

Had she tripped and fallen? Her shoes didn't have a good grip and she could have hit her head as she went down...

Or— had she been smashed with a rock or stick?

The dinner should have been a hilarious, joyful occasion, writers mellow after a day of writing, but we picked desultorily at our chicken Cordon Bleu. Marion arrived, as planned, at six, but she was hardly eating either.

And Bron was drinking wine. I was surprised when she extended her glass for Frederick to pour wine, and hoped she'd limit herself to one glass, but I soon stopped counting. Every time I looked, her glass seemed to be full and on its way to her mouth.

"Nope, Neil was safe and secure in the Toronto jail," Bron said, reaching for the wine bottle. "He can't be held responsible for Charlene. And the same goes for that hooker, Suzanne. There's another one they can't pin on old Neil!"

After coffee we retired to the lounge. Brandy might be a good idea, Roberta said. Soon everyone was ordering drinks and the mood lightened. Nobody felt like going to bed: we were waiting for news about Charlene's condition.

"It's might to be a long night," Frederick said.

"Awful thing."

"Terrible."

"So young."

"...brain damage..."

"Those paths can be tricky."

"I almost went down."

"...those shoes of hers."

"I'm too sensitive for violence." (Frances.)

"An accident. Who would want to harm her?"

Yes, an accident. That was the consensus, but after talk about accidents they had witnessed, bones they had broken, suddenly the conversation took a strange turn: which one of us could have done it? Who was where? Were there witnesses?

"Well, you're the mystery writer," Bella said to me. "You tell us what you think."

"I've forgotten how good this stuff tastes," Bron said to no one in particular. She was on her third brandy and she'd told me to mind my own business when I suggested the brandy after all the wine might not be such a good idea.

She drained her glass and stood up to get the bartender's attention. But there was Linda, looking nervously in our direction.

Were she and Bill worried about a lawsuit? I wondered. She had been nothing but sympathetic and efficient earlier, and Bill had driven Brad to the hospital, but the thought of a lawsuit must be crossing their minds, I thought as I waved her over.

"Sit down with us," I said. "We're playing whodunit."

I was a little tipsy myself: three glasses of wine, the brandy, and little food.

A look of commiseration passed between Marion and Linda. So I had been right about the idea of a lawsuit. Two years ago, a woman had fallen down the stairs at Marion's B & B and broken her arm. Lawyers' letters had come and gone...

"It has been one hell of a day," I told Linda as she squeezed between Marion and Amanda, who had been talking between themselves.

"Let us get sleuthing," Frederick said, producing the small notebook he always carried in his pocket.

It soon turned out that no one, with the exception of Roberta and Bella, who had been together on the porch of the cabin, had an alibi. Even Marsha and Betsy had split up later in the afternoon, each having a nap in her own room.

"Even I could have been the guilty one," Frederick claimed as Bron lurched, then ran, in the direction of the washroom.

Damn it all to hell! She wanted another drink! She would have another drink! She cried, shaking off my arm. Her eyes were bleary, unfocused, and her face was red and flushed. As she veered away from me, her hip struck the corner of the vanity and she would have fallen if I hadn't steadied her.

The door slammed behind her.

What now?

She'd left her large purse on the floor. I picked it up and followed her.

"No, I don't need any coffee! Gimme a beer! Haven't had a beer yet!" she was crying to Linda, who shook her head at the bartender. Bron noticed and set out for the bar.

"Poor thing," Amanda said. "I didn't know she'd had so much. She'll be embarrassed in the morning."

"Won't remember," Bella said. "Won't remember a thing."

Dealing with Bron wasn't pretty. She swore at Linda, cried, tried to kiss the bartender, and then she asked Frederick if he thought she was drunk. She wasn't drunk, she wasn't! We were just a bunch of fuddy-duddies!

Finally she agreed to go outside for a cigarette. She wanted a smoke, didn't she?

"I'll bum one from you," Linda told her, "and then we'll see about a beer."

Finally, finally, two cigarettes later, we got Bron to her room, where she immediately flopped backwards onto the bed and closed her eyes.

"I don't like this," Linda said. "She shouldn't go to sleep with so much alcohol in her system. She could vomit and choke to death. Oh, the joys of being an innkeeper, Carolyn. It's not all fun and games."

"What should we do?"

We stood looking at Bron, who was already snoring.

"After what happened today, I'm inclined to send her to the hospital," Linda said.

"Oh, no!" I thought of how devastated Bron would be to wake up and find herself in the hospital.

"We can't leave her alone," Linda said as Bill came in. He agreed with Linda: Bron should go to the hospital.

"She's an alcoholic," I said. "She hasn't touched a drop in a long time. Until tonight. Can't I just stay with her? I'll sit up all night— you can send some coffee to Bron's room. She'd feel so awful, going to the hospital." And what if Maureen found out? "Please, I'll stay awake and watch her."

They weren't happy about my suggestion, but they agreed— reluctantly.

I don't know what fluke, what miracle, what perversion of nosiness made me, at two in the morning, after four cups of very strong coffee, look inside Bron's suitcase. I told myself I was looking for something to read as I opened her zippered tartan suitcase.

Best American Short Stories would provide enough reading, I told myself, but then I found something that was far more important.

Something that explained everything.

Chapter Twenty-Nine

Sitting up all night with Bron, who awoke, humiliated and ashamed, at seven, was the perfect excuse to sleep in, but I was too keyed up to close my eyes.

And too frightened.

"You look so-o-o tired," Amanda said, patting the seat beside her at breakfast.

The pretty table with the pink and white dishes, the pot of fall asters, looked skewered through my exhausted eyes. Larger than life. And the coffee seemed stronger than any I had ever had.

"You should get some sleep," Amanda went on.

"How's Bron?" Bella wanted to know. She was as flamboyantly made up as always, but her face looked tired.

"Sick and sorry. She'll be too ashamed to show her face. She had a shower and went back to bed. She'll be okay. She's had a problem for a long time. She hadn't had a drink in months and months before last night."

They listened sympathetically as I told them about Bron. Roberta and Betsy spoke about when they had gotten drunk years before and the conversation flowed, but it was hard to concentrate. I knew the truth now, but it seemed so improbable, so far-fetched... I closed my eyes and opened them and the china shimmered and the morning sunlight coming through the windows hung in the air.

"How is Charlene?" I asked. "Has anyone heard?"

She was going to make it. She had been up-listed from "critical" to "serious." Bill had talked to Brad at the hospital.

And the police had more questions.

"I'm going to have a shower after breakfast," I said, "and then I thought we could meet at the big cabin by eleven-thirty."

"Are you sure you feel up to it?" Amanda asked. "Are you all right?"

"I'm all right."

But my knees shook when I stood up.

Everyone was at the cabin by eleven-thirty. It was the "big" cabin, but even so, it was crowded, and Betsy and Marsha perched on the braided rug in front of the hearth. There was no fire this morning, and the air was chilly, but Linda had supplied jugs of coffee and tea and soon everyone had their fingers wrapped around a warm cup.

"Everyone" did not include Bron, who had wanted to come. ("I have to face them sooner or later. If I don't come now, I won't return to the class," she told me.) "Trust me," I told her. "I have a good reason for you to stay away."

"Well, then," I began. "This retreat hasn't turned out the way I'd hoped. I'm sorry you won't have all pleasant memories of this weekend, but..."

I looked around the room. Did they suspect something? It seemed to me they were extra alert, waiting, or perhaps it was my voice, which sounded unreal even to me. Through the window, I saw a blue canoe on the calm lake. Red maples were mirrored on the water, and Bill was sitting on the edge of the dock.

"I thought a story would pull us together, remind us why we're here: because we're writers."

And so, I began reading Bron's story, from the copy I had found in her suitcase.

The manuscript was titled, "Stories and Lies."

It was a copy done in draft print, not in the near-letter quality of the good copies I had left, yesterday, in the dining room when I went for a walk. Bron's stories had only been unattended for half an hour, but that was plenty of time.

The good copy of the story I found in Bron's suitcase was missing from the file.

Someone had removed the story I would read now.

"And after I read Bron's story," I interrupted myself, "there should be time for some more readings of work you did yesterday."

And then I really did begin Bron's story:

Another weekend and there's Neil's car in the driveway. The washer has overflowed and the repairman didn't come as promised. Neil will have to drive me to the laundromat, I think, as he opens the door and Maureen runs into his arms.

This is in our little white house near London, the house near the railway tracks. The train comes by every morning at ten. People see me and I see them and I wonder about them and what they think of me. Sometimes I am hanging the wash or throwing a ball for Maureen. Once the train went by when I was spanking Maureen. I don't remember her misdeed now, but she was hollering and I had her over my knee and then the train went by and I saw a man's shocked face. Just that— shocked eyes, a dark beard, his disapproval.

The train also came by at eleven at night. I would lie awake in bed and listen to the rumbling, the whoosh of the wheels and think: how would it be to be going somewhere far away?

But I wasn't thinking of the train when Neil came home. I was worrying about the laundromat and Neil's displeasure at having to drive me. I sometimes thought of what Ann Landers said, how you should primp and make yourself nice for your husband when he came home, and have the kids scrubbed shiny clean, but I could somehow never manage this.

("She's changed tenses," I remarked.)

"Daddy, Daddy, we have to go to the laundromat right away!" Maureen told him before I could break the news gently about the broken washer.

To my surprise, Neil didn't fuss. He sighed and said we'd go after dinner and then he surprised me: why not go out to eat????!!!

So we loaded the car with the laundry and went for pizza and Neil seemed—different. Preoccupied. He didn't want to go to the laundromat, but he drove me, and while our sheets and towels were swooshing around, he went to the liquor store and bought a bottle of whiskey. I could smell the whiskey on his breath when he loaded the car with the laundry bags, and later I found out that he'd sat in the car, drinking and thinking, while Maureen was running a toy truck around the laundromat and I was reading "Can This Marriage Be Saved?" in Ladies' Home Journal.

Neil didn't talk to me the rest of the night. He drank the whiskey and he was still sitting there when I went to bed. He slept most of the next day, although I pestered him. "Get up! I'm alone all week! How dare you come home and not talk to me!"

I wanted his stories, you see. Nothing happened to me all week, except for the train going by.

Now I'm going to tell you how I remembered to tell this story. At my daughter Maureen's I came across a box of old clippings she had saved. They were my clippings, but she had kept them, and I did not remember this story until I saw the old, yellowed newspaper item I had cut out.

Neil showed it to me on Sunday, after we had a big fight. And this is what happened to Neil, in Toronto. They had set up a sting operation to catch men who were buying sex from hookers. The hookers and their pimps, mostly their pimps, were involved with drugs, and the police had a policewoman pretend to be a hooker.

It is Friday night in Toronto, near Eaton's downtown, and the young policewoman, wearing a black mini skirt and tight top and high heels, is strutting her stuff, when a well-dressed, middle-aged man approaches her and offers her fifty dollars.

Out come the cops. "Police!" they yell and proceed to arrest the man. They put the handcuffs on and the man collapses with a heart attack. But here is the worst part. As they are waiting for an ambulance and giving the man CPR, the man's daughter comes running across the street!

The man died. I do not have to say that Neil felt guilty. The girl cried and cried, he said, and just as they were putting the man in the ambulance, a newspaper photographer came along.

When I think about this man who died, I think of the man on the train who looked so disapproving and sad when I was spanking Maureen. Because all is chance: a good man who approached a hooker on a whim the same afternoon while his daughter, unbeknownst to him, decided to meet him after work. Another good man, on a train, sees a woman spanking a child and that is the image he will have of her forever.

"I've got the clipping to show you," I finished, "but what do you think happens years later?"

"The girl resents the cops," Bella said. "I sure would."

"They should legalize prostitution," Betsy said from the floor. "Then there wouldn't be any pimps."

"And disease would be controlled," Frederick said.

I looked up and saw Bron in the doorway.

"I want to apologize to everyone," she said. "Carolyn said I didn't have to come this morning, but I want to say how sorry I am. As you probably realize by now, I'm an alcoholic and last night I fell off the wagon."

"Sit down," Marsha said kindly. "There's room beside me. I'll just move over. We understand, Bron."

"You're among friends," Frederick said.

"I've just read them your story about Neil and the hooker in Toronto," I told Bron.

"It's uneven. I wasn't going to put it with the others. I know the ending is weak. And I need more dialogue."

"It wasn't with the others, Bron. I left your stories in the dining room and someone removed that one. I found another copy in your suitcase last night. I'm afraid I snooped."

Bron shrugged.

"Did you ever hear the end of the story?" I asked her. "Like, what happened to the man's daughter?"

"No. I forgot all about her until I found the clipping. Maureen saved all that old stuff from home."

"Here's how I see the ending," I said. I didn't look at anyone. "The girl grows up and has this great and deep resentment for the policeman she blames for her father's death. When she's older she tracks him down. It's not too hard. She has a copy of the newspaper photo; there's an inquest where she learns the officer's name.

"She stalks him after her mother dies. Her mother has to die first. The mother's ill, you see, a great burden, but the mother's death releases the daughter.

"So, she finds the policeman and decides to ruin his life as she feels he has ruined hers. Her hatred has been building. Killing him would be too easy, and it would end the thing, too. She's an intelligent and creative woman. She likes plotting, imagining scenarios. She wants to write the script about how to ruin his life.

"She finds him working in a small town and befriends a woman who is working at the police detachment. The woman is lonely, a misfit, and also hates the police, who, in the distant past, charged her father with growing dope. She is convinced that this has wrecked her father's life. Her mother always throws this up to the father, you see. And she's afraid the pot charge might prevent the girl from getting a permanent staff job with the police force."

I didn't dare to raise my eyes. Had anyone guessed?

"And she persuades this woman, somehow, that the policeman raped her."

"I don't believe that." Roberta's voice. "You don't persuade someone to make up a story like that."

"I don't know how she did it, but she did it," I said.

"She could have made up stories about the policeman saying bad things about the girl— the other girl, the one who worked at the station," Greg Theriault said. "Like, she was a real dog. That she smelled. That would piss anyone off."

"That's good," I said. "Good thinking. Okay, so the woman says she was raped, but then she gets scared. She doesn't want to play along; the thing's grown too complicated. She wants to forget the whole thing."

Helena would want to leave town, I thought. I could imagine her saying, "Well, you carry the ball now. See what you can do." Or, more probably: "I don't know if I want to continue this or not. Maybe I should refer people to you."

That was like the Helena who made complications over Mrs. Dalby's *Prairie Fire.*

"And so...

"It's a made-up story," I said. "But it's based on something real. Do you want to see the clipping?"

I looked at Amanda. She was fumbling in her purse.

But she wasn't stupid. She wasn't going to pull a gun on me in front of so many people.

And she didn't run away. She even passed the clipping along, after glancing at it, and why should she worry? In the photo, her face was made up for her cosmetic counter job.

Our eyes met. Hers gave nothing away.

"But how did this woman get the policeman's gun which killed the girl crying rape?" I asked, then answered my own question. "She had a drink with him, doctored his, and somehow stole his car keys. She wasn't expecting to find the gun in his car. Maybe she wasn't even planning to kill the other woman. But the gun was there and she took it. It was... something she had fantasized about. It wasn't real. Even when she pressed the trigger, it wasn't real. It didn't happen, as far as she was concerned. She wiped the gun on her coat and threw it into the bushes. She was thinking about her mother at the time, telling herself stories inside her head. Wonderful stories..."

Amanda stared.

"You could write that story," I told her. "Write about remembering the mother as the woman's body crumpled and fell backwards."

Amanda smiled.

And walked out of the cabin.

No one spoke. As one, we crowded the doorway and watched as she strolled down to the lake. Bill was still sitting there, but he turned when we yelled, a great chorus of "Watch it! Look out!" as Amanda took a gun out of the pocket of her voluminous skirt.

Instinctively, Bill put up an arm, and as shots echoed, he fell backwards into the lake.

Amanda kept firing— at the dock, at rocks and trees— until the cartridge was empty.

Not Jane, who had merely wanted to find out the truth about Helena; not an unknown thug; not a criminal from the past.

But Amanda, my star writer, the head of the class, tomorrow's CanLit wonder.

Tatiana.

Epilogue

From the cabin that has become my writing studio, I can see the dock now. A board has to be replaced, but next year we're putting in a new and larger dock. It's spring and the leaves are just coming out, although today, as I write this, it's raining; but rain, I have always found, is conducive to writing.

I am thinking about Amanda and her story— her story and her long memory with its passions and secrets, the dark and hidden obsession that motivated her life. Even her writing? No, no; I refuse to believe that. Her writing and talent stand apart; the talent didn't grow out of that darkness.

I can see Amanda as a young girl, intelligent and imaginative.

A young woman with plans, a good student devoted to her father, who made her life a pleasure, despite the irrational mother. A sane, adult mind would not have blamed the undercover cop who caught her father with a prostitute. But a sensitive, adolescent person— with perhaps a touch of the mother's madness?— had grasped this idea of blame. Alone with her mother, day after day... I could picture a younger Amanda slamming pot lids and banging doors and yelling. No university, no tomorrow, just a bank job and more yelling and craziness when she came home at night.

Amanda awake until two, three, in the morning, turning the thing around in her mind. Waking up with a puffy face, splashing on the cold water, taking the subway to the bank. Another humdrum day. She's a thin woman with an unremarkable face. She greets customers: smile, smile; she forces herself to memorize facts from the courses, but her head pounds. Sometimes she thinks she will strangle her mother. Or run away, not return from the bank, but go to the airport and catch a flight to Europe.

But working in a bank has an advantage: the computer with its access to customers' bank accounts. She knew his name; typed it into the computer regularly and found nothing. And then, one day, around the time he started living with Jane, the name Neil Andersen made an appearance on her computer screen. He had purchased an RRSP, transferred some money...

This knowledge was a candle glowing in the dark cave. And why not drive by his house, follow him? A drive-by visit, a hang-up phone call: the candle burned brighter, opening vistas and possibilities. Now the man who, she felt, had ruined her life, had stepped out of dreams and thoughts and become real. She found out where he had his hair cut, how often he mowed the grass, where he had his car serviced. She discovered the doughnut shop he went to and saved his empty paper cup.

Meeting Helena in Leicester, where Jane had followed Neil, enabled Amanda to learn more. Amanda found out about his western roots, that his father was dead. Helena told her that onion rings gave Neil indigestion, that he took vitamin C for a cold, that he couldn't find the warranty slip for his television set, that he had broken his favourite coffee mug.

This knowledge fueled the half-formed ideas of revenge. Why not create chaos in Neil's life, as he had created chaos in hers? Helena had a crush on Neil? Why not convince her that Neil returned her feelings? Neil had driven Helena home? His hand had accidentally brushed against Helena's hand? He had seemed reluctant to drive off? Well, then. Those dreams Helena had about Neil meant something. Amanda was sure that

Neil returned Helena's feelings, but perhaps he was held back by Helena's father's old criminal charge? Hmmm...

It was easy for Amanda to turn Helena's attraction for Neil into bitterness. Neil was just a cop. He had no sympathy for Wilbur. And what about those dreams? Was Helena sure there wasn't more to the dreams? Hadn't Neil led her on? And was Helena sure nothing had happened? Had she blocked something out? What about Neil's live-in girlfriend? What? Helena didn't know that the girlfriend was this sexy blonde? Did Helena want to see the girlfriend? Yes? Amanda and Helena had driven to Guelph and watched Jane planting flowers in the garden. Helena cried, then raged.

"Neil's no good at all," Amanda told Helena.

For Amanda, directing Helena was simple: it was like writing a story, and she was good at making up stories. I could see Amanda earnestly leaning forward, listening to Helena (and who else paid attention to Helena?); could imagine the late-night talk fests, going over and over the story, discussing Neil's actions and motivations. His faults grew with the telling, were multiplied and magnified with repetition.

Helena was a godsend to Amanda. And her pitfall, too, because once the scenario was in place, the story, like all good stories, had a life of its own. Yes, Helena agreed, Neil was rotten, the worst there was. It was true, she'd had dreams, feelings, suspicions: perhaps he really did rape her and she had blocked it out of her mind? Was that possible? She didn't want to lose Amanda's friendship— "Tatiana's" friendship...

But if stories have lives of their own, so do the characters in them. After Helena moved to Toronto, she spoke openly about the rape to the women at the Women's Centre. A new chapter began, a dangerous one filled with publicity and legalities. And behind Helena's shyness lay slyness and wariness. Sneakiness. She had had enough. "I could say it was all your idea," Helena told Amanda.

But for Amanda, revenge was too close. The story had almost written itself. How could the story end with nothing happening? She wasn't going to let that occur.

The story happened much as I told it to my writing group that day in the cabin. Amanda did drug Neil's drink. I myself had told her that Neil was going to drive Juliana to the airport! All Amanda had to do was to find out the time of departure for Juliana's flight, wait for Neil at the airport, and follow him around Toronto to the Quartet. She did find the gun in his car, and yes, she hadn't planned to kill Helena. She had planned to do something, somehow, and when the gun presented itself— unsought, unlooked for, a surprise: she had taken it. She had her own gun, obtained years before, but Neil's gun was another surprise in the series of surprises she discovered following Neil around.

Always in disguise. Sometimes she dressed as a vamp, sometimes as a man.

And Amanda had killed Mrs. Maloff, who threatened to call the police when she saw Amanda going into Neil's house after she had taken the spare key from its hiding place under the loose patio stone where she had glimpsed Bron replacing it. Amanda had been late for class that night; she had waited down the street until I picked Bron up before trying to enter Neil's house. It wouldn't have been the first time she poked around in there, but this time Mrs. Maloff was taking her garbage out.

So Burton was right: he had seen someone hanging around, and this was the information Suzanne had wanted to tell me. I am convinced, today, that Suzanne recognized Amanda following Neil and put two-and-two together after she saw me with Amanda— at the Walper, or at the restaurant in Kitchener.

Amanda hit Charlene, whom she recognized from the bank where she worked in Toronto. It was an unnecessary assault. Charlene, when she recovered, said she had not remembered Amanda.

Luckily, Bill was only slightly hurt, with a superficial shot to the arm. I think that after the first shot, Amanda just kept shooting at nothing. Impulse, craziness: the story I related had recalled the shooting of Helena: how easy it had been. She had to fire a gun again, that was all.

Amanda had written everything down in her wonderful and creative way. She had detailed the information I had given her, had notes on Neil's financial records from the bank's computer, had pondered about Charlene, who had been less than friendly that night at the Walper— catty, even. Hitting Charlene puzzled me until I learned from Amanda's notebooks that she thought Charlene knew that Amanda had been reprimanded at the bank for taking extra time off— days when she was in Leicester with Helena. Amanda had rented a room in a bed and breakfast in Leicester, and her frequent absences from work had caused problems with her supervisor.

Before the police took her away, Amanda handed me her apartment keys and smiled in that unreal way she had shown in the cabin during the reading of Bron's story.

"Look after my stories," Amanda said, and while it is true that two police officers accompanied me, it was I who found her stories— her memoirs— in her desk, in her own handwriting. I read quickly, before the police removed the notebooks as evidence, but not before realizing however much she needed to keep her revenge story a secret, the need to write the truth was greater...

The police discovered various wigs in the piano.

The police found, too, a whimpering, starving orange and white cat in the locked pantry. My Willy! She had stolen him from my place and locked him up, giving him a few scraps and water once or twice a week. (There was a poem about this: "The Sadder and Sadder Cat." The sadder and sadder cat who had scratched her, keeping her away from class the week she had "a cold.")

He was sadder and sadder, all right. He didn't remember me at first and crouched, hiding and shaking, behind a mattress, but I kept repeating his name, and suddenly he hurled himself against my neck.

He's purring beside me now, in the big yellow chair by the window.

"The day's work is done," I tell Willy, turning off the light and stopping outside to look back at my cabin, where my words are flowing once again. I think of Neil, restored to honour, and wonder how he is doing now that Bron has found a job in Toronto. All "my" writers are scheduled for another retreat, in June.

I carry Willy up the path. He's become a real suck, and as Conrad comes bounding towards us, barking in an insulted way— *Why do you bother with a CAT?*— Willy leans against me and his eyes search out mine: buddies forever.

We have come here together, to this place which is both new and old, where the future is still uncertain. I think it will be fine, but sometimes when there are no guests, when little is happening, I think of cities, of crowds, of anonymity.

But then I think of my grandmother's house. I did not sell it. Although it meant taking out a larger mortgage, we bought the lodge without the sale of my Maine property. And the idea of the house, my old home, being there for me, is an idea of a future which is not set, not clearly defined, but a future holding maybes and surprises.

In the lodge, I deposit my cat on the registration counter, where Peter is checking in tourists who have come for the trout fishing. The tourists, I always tell Peter, will think Willy the Greeter is a charming addition to an inn that has its own resident author, mother-in-law boss (Marion really organizes everything and I'm glad she does, so I can write) and a crazy yellow Lab who is getting fatter by the day because everyone feeds him.

"Welcome to Hall Manor," I tell the men. "This is Willy, the in-house cat."